James Douglas Jerrold Kelley

The Question of Ships' the Navy and the Merchant Marine

James Douglas Jerrold Kelley

The Question of Ships' the Navy and the Merchant Marine

ISBN/EAN: 9783337418892

Printed in Europe, USA, Canada, Australia, Japan

Cover: Foto ©Andreas Hilbeck / pixelio.de

More available books at **www.hansebooks.com**

THE QUESTION OF SHIPS

THE QUESTION OF SHIPS

THE NAVY AND THE MERCHANT MARINE

BY

J. D. JERROLD KELLEY

LIEUT. U. S. NAVY

NEW YORK
CHARLES SCRIBNER'S SONS
1884

With this contribution to the vexed question of ships I venture to associate the name of James Gordon Bennett, Esq., in grateful recognition of the truth, courage, and loyalty with which the NEW YORK HERALD *has sustained the cause of ships and sailors everywhere.*

J. D. J. K.

U. S. Naval Board of Inspection Foreign Vessels, New York City, January 31, 1884.

CONTENTS.

CHAPTER IX.

CHAPTER X.

CHAPTER XI.

The Question of Ships.

CHAPTER I.

OUR CHANCES FOR MARITIME SUCCESS.

IT is a curious fact that a great commercial question, vital in its influence upon the well-being of an eminently practical nation, should so often be approached upon the side of sentiment. A bewildering maze of statistics, an array of accommodating figures, and a dexterous spinning of subtle phrases, are made to form the premises, not of an irrefutable conclusion, but of an appeal, which fires the heart, if it do not satisfy the head, of many a patriot. To discuss a question so sober, so melancholy as the restoration of the Merchant Marine, from the standpoint of its poetical merits, is not *a priori* convincing of its imminent necessity; and, whether an advocate shines in the broad light-beam of free-trade, or is glorious in the panoply of protection, he should forswear heroics and pleas *ad hominem*, and treat the subject from the grossly material vantage-ground of dollars and cents.

There should be in the beginning, for example, a thorough understanding of the terms to be employed in the discussion : a spade should be called a spade, and mean nothing else ; the necessity and fitness for the possession of a merchant marine by any country should be proven, and not assumed ; the history and growth of the industry should be studied and compared; the causes of its decay should be formulated ; and then, as with an invalid after a careful diagnosis by a physician, the remedies should be prescribed. Sentiment can no more enter this problem than into the determination of the next eclipse ; and so far as the question permits, all its complex and interdependent conditions should be viewed and tested.

It is an axiom that the greatest good to the greatest number is secured, where trade and industrial questions are operative, when the whole population of a nation is engaged in those pursuits which pay best under the environment of the country. There is no imperative demand upon any people to possess a Carrying Trade, a Shipbuilding Industry, or a Foreign Commerce. The carrying trade is an occupation of men who own or control ships, and differs from shipbuilding as carting does from wagon-building ; looked at broadly, the two interests are hostile, because shipowners wish to buy new vessels at low prices, to keep the competing vessels few in number, to maintain freights at the highest figures, and to buy cheap, good ships without regard to the nationality or locality of the builder.

Foreign commerce is the exchange under varying conditions, the simpler the better, of the products of one country for those of another; merchants want plenty of competing ships, and low freights, and to them it is a matter of indifference by whom the

vessels are built, owned, or navigated.　In other
directions these interests are correlated, and each is
of great value ; but of all, commerce is the active
principle, for lacking it, a country needs neither to
own nor to build ships.　The carrying trade is an industry which, in itself, is neither more nor less desirable than any other, than shoemaking for instance : and it is engaged in only because, for equal
expenditure of labor and capital, more profit is
promised than by any other business.　Nor does it
follow, if a nation had a commerce, and certain of
its citizens found the carrying trade to be an advan-
tageous employment for their labor and capital as
compared with other industries, that other of its
citizens ought to engage in shipbuilding.　Any person may have a whim for owning a ship built in his
native country and be willing to pay for the gratifica-
tion its possession affords ; but if it costs him more
to do this than to buy abroad, he has lost money.
"A fisherman," as Professor Sumner quaintly puts
it, "who has caught nothing sometimes buys a fish
at a fancy price.　He saves himself mortification
and gets a dinner, but the possession of the fish does
not prove that he has profitably employed his time
or that he has had sport."

Should a country own a foreign trade it would not
necessarily be an object for it to do its own carrying,
any more than it would be an object for a farmer to
insist upon carting to market his own produce,
when some person regularly employed in that business offered him a contract on better terms than his
own.　Quite as foolish would the man be who refused to carry on a carting business unless he could

build his own wagons; and sunk in the deepest deeps is a nation which knows that certain of its citizens could buy and use carts so as to make a legitimate profit, and yet denies the privilege, because certain other equally as good citizens could not build similar carts at home for a profit.

Maritime success, or the possession of the elements which determine the fitness of a nation for marine enterprise, can no more be called a question of chance than can watchmaking; nor is there any uncertainty about the conditions which qualify a nation for eminence in navigation. It is subject to the same economic rules, and its genesis, development, and decay follow the same laws that underlie the evolution and growth of man. Certain impulses go to the establishment of these marine activities: if all exist, pre-eminence is assured; if some are wanting, there will be alternate periods of exaltation and of depression, and, possibly, of ultimate decadence; and if all or large numbers are absent, no outside aid, whether legislative or individual, can arrest the operations of the inevitable law. Trade may be forced, but all industries are nowhere less than contingent; and none of them can exist if certain natural conditions are lacking.

Briefly generalized, the first impulse towards maritime enterprise arises out of life in a region which will not support its inhabitants by agriculture—"original poverty of soil or limited extent of territory almost arising to the heights of a necessary qualification" (Hall). The born navigators of the world have always lived in little half-barren countries, situated in the midst of fruitful regions; the

almost invariable rule being that those who inhabit-
ed a rich soil never engaged in navigation until the
population became so dense that agriculture would
not afford sustenance to all.   This was the case with
the Carthagenians, the Greeks, the Latin races of Europe, the English, and among other people in America, the New-Englanders.   These last took to the
sea because the shore did not furnish them with
products which would remunerate their capital and
labor equally as well ; while on the other hand the
people of the Southern States clung to the fruitful
land, never fostered nor inherited a taste for the
ocean, and to-day do not own one-ninth of the ships
under our flag.

Ocean fisheries affect the maritime fitness of a
people by the training they give to sailors, and by
their encouragement and exercise of those qualities
which prepare mariners for the daring and difficult
enterprises of their calling ; in every age the fisheries have been the original temptations which induced men to go to sea, and the only nations that
have been eminent in shipping have fished from the
beginning.

It is an accepted law that an art-loving or an art-
producing community does not display energy in
commerce and industry ; a roaming disposition, a
love of adventure, a jealousy of participation in home
affairs by foreigners, and a spirit of traffic and industry, invariably impel in the direction of maritime
enterprise, and thus make it largely dependent upon
the genius of a people.

It is only a region situated in the midst of great
seas, and advantageously central, that can in the

long run have the most ships and be supreme in
commerce ; this, which was so potent in the past,
will have double significance in a future of general
settlement of inhabitable lands. The flag of commercial enterprise shifts with centres of civilization
and settlement ; and of two nations competing for
trade and navigation to a great market, that one in
the end will secure the larger share which is the
nearer or which has the better geographical position.

A great population and a large surplus of native
commodities are essential to the permanency and
greatness of a merchant marine. This does not pre-
clude a certain trade being built up by small nations
with a limited population and no commerce ; for, as
to-day in the North Countries, a people, forced from
irresistible conditions to follow the sea, might find
it profitable to prosecute a carrying trade ; but
under a limiting environment such an industry
would be rarely permanent and never great. The
wants and energies of a large native population develop trade ; and when the genius of a people is, as
with most nations, one-sided—agriculture as opposed
to manufacturing, for example—the laws of supply
and demand, and the exigencies growing out of the
ownership of a large surplus product, must insure
marine enterprise.

Abundant resources in material for ships ; economy in ship construction and operation ; capability
of production for a definite sum less than rival nations ; power, in the absence of this, of purchasing
where they are best and cheapest ; a wise policy of
government—these, and all of these, go to the making of the ideal commercial nation.

Do we then possess this fitness, this capacity for maritime success ? So far as commerce affects, this country has a vital interest in the carrying trade, let theorists befog the cool air as they may ; every dollar paid for freight imported or exported in American vessels accrues to American labor and capital, and the enterprise is as much a productive industry as the raising of wheat, the spinning of fibre, or the smelting of ore. Had the acquired, the " full " trade of 1860 been maintained without increase, $80,000,000 would have been added in 1880 to the national wealth, and the gain from diverted shipbuilding would have swelled this sum to a total of $160,000,000. Our surplus products must find foreign markets ; and to retain them, ships controlled by and employed in exclusively American interests are essential instrumentalities. Whatever tends to stimulate competition and to prevent combination benefits the producer ; and as the prices abroad establish values here, the barter we obtain for the despised one-tenth of exports—$665,000,000 in 1880—determines the profit or loss of the remainder in the home market. Is it generally known, for instance, that a difference in cost of a single penny in laying down grain at Liverpool may decide whether this product shall be drawn from the United States or from the agricultural districts of Hungary and Southern Russia ? During the last fiscal year 11,500,000 gross tons of grain, oil, cotton, tobacco, precious metals, etc., were exported from the United States, and this exportation increases at the rate of 1,500,000 tons annually ; 3,800,000 tons of goods are imported, or in all about 15,000,000 tons constitute the existing commerce of

this country. If only one-half of the business of
carrying our enormous wealth of surplus products
could be secured for American ships, our tonnage
would be instantly doubled, and we would have a
greater fleet engaged in a foreign trade, legitimately
our own, than Great Britain has to-day (Hall). The
United States makes to the ocean-carrying trade its
most valuable contribution, no other nation giving
to commerce so many bulky tons of commodities to
be transported those long voyages which in every
age have been so eagerly coveted by maritime peoples.

If the larger proportion of this commerce consisted in articles of foreign growth and manufacture,
it would not be strange to find foreign ships securing the larger share of the business ; but of the
17,000 ships which enter and clear at American ports
every year, 4,600 seek a cargo empty, and but 2,000
sail without obtaining it. Trade is largely governed
by the social, industrial and economical conditions
of the consumer. A careful study of the commercial
relations of the British colonies of Australia, New
Zealand, and South Africa demonstrates that with
them, notwithstanding the competition of the
mother-country, there are splendid opportunities
yet untried ; last year the imports of the two former reached a total of $400,000,000, and their neces-
sities demand the very articles we make most skil-
fully and supply most cheaply ; and for return
cargoes, Australia and the others have many things
we want cheap and are forced to buy dear. In 1879
the former sent to England wool valued at $35,000,000
and in the next year we imported from England

$23,760,000 of the same staple, obviously buying the Australian wool at second-hand for double freights and brokerages.

Ships are profitable abroad, and can be made profitable here ; and, in truth, during the last thirty years no other branch of industry has made such progress as the carrying trade. To establish this there are four points of comparison—commerce, railways, shipping tonnage, and carrying power of the world—limited, for the sake of illustration, to the years between 1850 and 1880.

	1850.	1880.	Increase. per cent.
Commerce of all nations..	$4,280,000,000	$14,405,000,000	240
Railways—miles open...	44,400	222,000	398
Shipping tonnage.......	6,905,000	18,720,000	171
Carrying tonnage.......	8,464,000	34,280,000	304

In 1850, therefore, for every $5,000,000 of international commerce there were 54 miles of railway, and a maritime carrying power of 9,900 tons ; and in 1880 the respective ratios had risen to 77 miles and 12,000 tons ; this has saved one-fourth freight, and brought producer and consumers into such contact that we no longer hear " of the earth's products being wasted, of wheat rotting in La Mancha, of wool being used to mend roads in Paraguay, and of sheep being burnt for fuel in making bricks in the Argentine Republic." England has mainly profited by this enormous development, the shipping of the United Kingdom earning $300,000,000 yearly, and employing 200,000 seamen, whose industry is therefore equivalent to £300 per individual, as compared with £190 gained by each of the factory operatives. The

freight earned by all flags for sea-borne merchandise
is $500,000,000 or about 8 per cent. of the value
transported.   Hence the toll which all nations pay
to England for the carrying trade is equal to 4 per
cent. (nearly) of the exported values of the earth's
products and manufactures ; and pessimists who declare that ship-owners are losing money or making
small-profits must be wrong, for the merchant marine is expanding every year.

What then is our situation ? We have been a
great maritime nation, therefore we must have had
some of the qualities essential to success ; we have
had a great commerce, a great shipbuilding interest,
and a great carrying trade, hence our citizens must
have found these industries profitable.   The national
genius for trade, adventure, and enterprise has become intensified by the changes modern life demands ; our fisheries are still profitable, whaling
(owing to the petroleum production) alone excepted ; every year our geographical position has
improved, so that now we are the Great Middle
Kingdom ; our national resources in nearly every
direction have quadrupled ; our population, swelled
last year by 600,000 emigrants, is so dense that our
eastern coasts are overcrowded with people whose
race requirements—sea-coast born or descended, as
opposed to inland reared—demand a sea environment ; the carrying trade was never more profitable ;
our commerce has expanded so enormously that it is
not only a question of profit but of serious necessity
that we should manage it, from the growing of the
blade to its freighting in every sea—and yet, with
every impulse, every activity insisting that we should

assume our place in the world, our Merchant Marine
is in a state of decadence.   Our people are not more
profitably employed in other occupations, and therefore it must be in bad laws, apathy of government,
or the lack of special resources that the causes will
be discovered.

CHAPTER II.

RISE AND FALL OF OUR COMMERCE.

THE first vessels built upon our shores were intended exclusively for the fisheries and the coasting trade, the pioneer merchants being contented with the quick returns and small profits of a commerce that was not controlled by exacting foreign governments. The vessels were necessarily small, and, though admirably fitted for their work, of the type struggling shipbuilders must perforce produce. As early as 1660 the fisheries off our coast had become so valuable that as many as six hundred sails were found upon the Banks during a season, and so great were the profits that the boats often paid for themselves in one voyage. Gaining confidence by successful rivalry in a trade which foreigners had aggrandized, the New England merchants extended their enterprises in other directions, and, before the Revolutionary War, they had built up a commerce which was substantially profitable not only on our own coast, but with Europe and the Spanish West Indies.

The war naturally checked the growth of navigation ; but, as a compensation, shipbuilding acquired so great an impetus from privateering, that when peace was established, there were nowhere more skilled or more intelligent ship-designers and mechanics than our own. At this time our shipping could not have exceeded 100,000 tons, though, as the government had no control over the registry until after the adoption of the Constitution, no definite knowledge is attainable. Foreigners, however, still controlled the best part of our trade, for at that time "the prominent fact," writes Hall, "was the preponderance of European bottoms in the foreign trade ; in 1789 the registration was 123,893 tons ; 68,607 in the coasting trade ; 9,062 in the fisheries ; and there were still 100,000 tons of foreign shipping in the external commerce." The active social, political, and economic principle of each nation in those days was eminently not fair dealing to other people ; and the accepted theory of trade among the stronger nations was the imposition of such burdens upon the weaker maritime countries that the latter were certain to be driven from all but home ports. The new United States suffered particularly by this policy ; and upon her entrance in the race of the trading nations, asserted as cardinal principles growing out of her political aspirations, freedom of commerce and entire reciprocity of intercourse.

Treaties were sought, but in vain, until 1782, when the Dutch, after four years of negotiation initiated by Franklin and consummated by John Adams, signed a convention which gave the ships of both nations exact reciprocity in the ports of each other. At the close of the Revolutionary War an attempt was made to enter into a similar treaty with England, but after a vexatious delay of several years, not only was the offer rejected, but a policy more severe than that shown to any of the European governments was adopted towards the new Re-

public. In July, 1789, the first Congress under the
Constitution passed the celebrated Navigation Act,
which, coming as it did from a weak country, im-
perilling a shipping unprotected by an adequate
naval force, excited in Europe a most profound as-
tonishment. That its enactment in part was retalia-
tory of England's attitude was never doubted, and
at first there were threats that boded ill for the kin
across the sea ; then came doubts, not of justice but
of expediency; accentuated by the increasing ap-
pearances of American ships in foreign waters ; and
finally negotiations, controversies, and treaties ; these
at first with England in 1794, then with Spain in
1795, and at last with France in 1800.

Though the provisions of these treaties were not
entirely satisfactory, yet they were movements in a
right direction ; and so much was commerce stimulated that in 1800 seven-eighths of the freights was
carried in American ships ; the home trade with
China was exclusively our own ; and between 1798
and 1812, 200,000 tons of shipping beyond our
needs were sold to foreigners. "Secure in the protection of our laws . . . our merchants entered
upon the present century a class of prosperous men
and full of confident anticipations for the future "
(Hall). Shipping had increased in tonnage as follows :

Years.	Registered for Foreign Trade.	Coasting Trade.	Fisheries.
1789	123,893	68,607	9,062
1795	529,470	164,795	34,102
1800	669,921	246,295	30,078
1805	749,341	301,366	58,363

England, unable outside of protocols to look upon

us as anything but rebellious colonists, still subjected our ships to such annoying visits and im-
pressed so many of our seamen that, in twelve years,
our merchants suffered great losses by the detention
and crippling of their vessels—no less than 6,000 men
having been forcibly taken from the decks under our
flag.   A further interference with our commerce resulted from the blockade of the coasts of France and
of the Netherlands, and from the subsequent publica-
tion of the Berlin Decree and of the English Orders
in Council of 1806, and from the Milan Decree of
1807 ; in consequence of these necessities of foreign
war, over 1660 American ships were captured, and
either condemned with their cargoes or subjected to
great losses by trade interference, high insurances
and delays ; many of our vessels were forced to seek
neutral harbors for protection, and were not only
seized at sea, but were searched at the mouths of
our own harbors.   America protested in vain, and
finally passed the Embargo Act.   In May, 1810,
France repealed the Berlin and Milan Decrees, but
Great Britain refused either to desist from her ob-
noxious policy of search, or to remove the prohibitions which forbade our ships seeking markets on
the free coasts of Western Europe.

   As a very natural result the war of 1812 followed ;
it cost the government $150,000,000 ; it destroyed on
land and sea thousands of lives and millions of private property, and at its close left us nearly bankrupt.
In 1810 our tonnage was 1,385,000, and on January 1,
1815, its gross amount was only 1,828,000 tons,—an
increase of less than 100,000 tons annually ; in three
years 2,300 of the enemy's vessels were captured,

"but our privateers destroyed many of these, and 750 were retaken, and we in turn lost 1,407 of our own merchant vessels and fishing boats, so that the balance was slightly in our favor." At last, in 1815, England made a commercial treaty; and though poor in resources, yet strong with the instincts of a young and vigorous life, the nation entered the great race for maritime supremacy, fortified by the knowledge of its past, by the justice of a present gained by blood and iron, and by the hopes of a future pregnant with promise.

As a matter of policy, Congress, in 1817, substantially re-enacted the navigation laws of England; our coasting trade was prohibited to other nations; ships in the foreign trade, unless two-thirds manned by Americans, were taxed fifty cents a ton; and the great quadrangular trade of Great Britain to Brazil, the East Indies, United States and England, was cut off. At the same time a frank offer of general reciprocity was made in which America proposed to put commerce upon the high plane of fraternity among nations, and to leave all victories within that field of action to the intelligence and enterprise of the different peoples of the world. This was declined; and it was not until 1830, and after more difficulties with England and France, that we had direct trade and reciprocity with the principal commercial nations.

From the peace of 1815 our commerce expanded in an extraordinary manner, increasing in money from $270,000,000 in that year to $480,000,000 in 1836; the annual travel and immigration rose from 20,000 to 75,000; and fifteen years later, in 1850, the ocean traffic of the United States gave employment to 2,335,000 tons of shipping—the total tonnage entering and clearing from our ports being 8,000,000. Nothing could supply more absolute proof of our fitness for the demands that a maritime industry imposes than this victory over forces and circumstances, which in every disguise and under every opposing condition met us at each forward essay.

Beginning at the end of the line, without a helping hand or an encouraging voice ; against obstacles that seemed insuperable ; in war; during a neutrality that was worse than actual belligerency; when harassed and fettered by cruel foreign impositions and discriminations, and impeded by the mistaken views of internal factions—yet, at the last, breasting the waves that were unbroken by rival keels, if not at the very head, yet missing it by so slight a degree that our coequality was recognized—surely never before since the world began was there such a record, never such testimony to the genius and instincts of a people. A widening field of commerce, followed by equality of competition, aided us ; the assertion of fair trading and of equal rights, emphasized by the splendid services of our navy, gave us a further claim to be heard ; our mariners were the best in the world, and our ships, notwithstanding the higher wages paid, were navigated the most economically ; our packet lines to Europe crossed in an average of less than twenty days, and American buyers could insure their goods in this country under the stipulation they should come in certain American ships ; the British whale fisheries were extinct, while ours employed over 700 ships and

17,000 seamen; in thirty years this country built 3,900,000 tons of shipping; all the mails and passengers and a large majority of the immigrants were transported under our flag; three-fourths of the cotton was exported in the same way, and best of all, the policy of the government was so aggressive that our flag was respected everywhere, and in certain trades, even under unequal conditions, had the preference over all competitors.

But from this period dates our decadence.

The maximum tonnage of this country at any time registered in the foreign trade was in 1861, and then amounted to 5,539,813 tons; Great Britain in the same year owning 5,895,369 tons, and all the other nations 5,800,767 tons. Between 1855 and 1860 over 1,300,000 American tons in excess of the country's needs were employed by foreigners in trades with which we had no legitimate connection save as carriers. In 1851 our registered steamships had grown from the 16,000 tons of 1848 to 63,920 tons—an amount almost equal to the 65,920 tons of England; and in 1855 this had increased to 115,000 tons and reached a maximum, for in 1862 we had 1,000 tons less. In 1855 we built 388 vessels, in 1856 306 vessels, and in 1880 26 vessels—all for the foreign trade. The total tonnage which entered our ports in 1856 from abroad amounted to 4,464,038, of which American built ships constituted 3,194,375 tons, and all others but 1,259,762 tons. In 1880 there entered from abroad 15,240,534 tons, of which 3,128,374 tons were American, and 12,112,000 were foreign—that is, in a ratio of 75 to 25, or actually 65,901 tons less than when we were twenty-four

years younger as a nation. This decadence did not
originate in the war between the States, but dates
from 1856, when it was detected in the decrease of
sales to foreigners—65,000 tons having been transferred in 1855, 42,000 in 1856, 26,000 in 1858, and
17,000 in 1860. In 1879 we built 43,000 tons of registered vessels, but at the same time we relinquished
148,000 tons ; this loss of 105,000 tons being distributed in 37,000 tons sold to foreigners (old vessels), 24,000 tons abandoned, and 87,000 tons lost.
The grain fleet, sailing in 1880 from the port of New
York, numbered 2,897 vessels, of which 1,822 were
sailing vessels carrying 59,822,033 bushels, and 1,075
were steamers laden with 42,426,533 bushels, and
among all these *there were 74 American sailing vessels
and not one American steamer*.

In 1856 the total exports and imports $641,604,850,
and in 1880 $1,613,770,663. In the first named year
there were carried in ships built, owned, manned
and commanded by Americans $482,268,274, and by
foreigners $153,336,516 ; in 1880 Americans trans-
ported $280,005,497, and foreigners $1,309,466,596 ;
the percentage of our carrying in our own trade was
in 1856, 75.2 ; and in 1880, 17.4.[1]

---

[1] Our domestic marine consists of about 25,211 vessels, aggregating 4,169,600 tons. Of this number 17,042 are sailing, 4,569 are
steam, 1,206 are canal boats, and 2,395 are barges. With respect
to location they are distributed as follows : The Atlantic and Gulf
coasts have 14,762 sailing vessels, aggregating 1,967,023 tons ; 2,-
162 steam vessels, 615,039 tons ; 658 canal boats, 58,963 tons ;
764 barges, 159,041 tons. The Pacific coast has 807 sailing vessels, 148,712 tons ; 308 steam, 107,040 tons ; 87 barges, 14,595
tons. The Northern Lakes have 1,473 sailing, 307,077 tons ; 896

In the general trade of the world our record is as
lamentable. "At the beginning of the 19th century," writes Yeats, "the commerce of the world
seemed passing into American hands, their shipping
having increased fivefold in twenty years." " Their
decline," continues Mulhall, " in recent years is un-
paralleled, as appears from the aliquot carrying
power belonging to various flags.

Country.	1850.	1870.	1880.
Great Britain	41	44	49
United States	15	8	6
France	8	8	7
Other flags	36	40	38

"In size of ships America has now reached the
mean attained by England in 1870, the average tonnage of all sea-going vessels afloat being in 1880 177
tons, or an increase in ten years of 36 per cent. in
medium tonnage." Our relative position is shown
exactly in the following table :

Country.	1870.	1880.	Increase, tons.
British	549	748	199
French	210	320	110
German	220	250	30
American	405	560	155
Norwegian	143	190	47
Italian	135	156	21

While this poison of decay has been eating into our
vitals, the possibilities of the country in nearly every
other industry have reached a plane of development

---

steam, 203,298 tons ; 549 canal boats, 44,774 tons ; 170 barges,
42,226 tons. The Western Rivers have 1,203 steam, 250,793 tons ;
1,373 barges, 251,015 tons.

beyond the dreams of the most enthusiastic theorizers ; we have spread out in every direction, and the promise of the future beggars imaginations attuned even to the key of our present and past development.

	1830.	1880.
Population	12,000,000.	50,000,000.
Railways	23 miles.	8,000 miles.
Cotton	976,000 bales.	5,500,000 bales.
Telegraphs	none.	100,000 miles.
Post-offices	8,000.	40,000.

	1840.	1880.
Wheat	84,000,000 bushels.	460,000,000 bushels.
Wool	35,000,000 pounds.	225,000,000 pounds.
Cotton Spindles	2,000,000.	10,000,000.

We have a timber area of 560,000,000 acres, and across our Canadian border there are 900,000,000 more acres ; and in coal and iron production we are approaching the old world.

		1842.	1879.
Coal	Great Britain	35,000,000 tons.	135,000,000 tons.
	United States	2,000,000 "	60,000,000 "
Iron	Great Britain	2,250,000 "	6,300,000 "
	United States	564,000 "	2,742,000 "

During these thirty-seven years the relative increase has been in coal from 300 to 2,900 per cent. ; in iron from 200 to 400 per cent., and all in our favor. But this is not enough, for England, with a coal area less than that of either Pennsylvania or Kentucky, has coaling stations in every part of the world, and our steamers cannot reach our Pacific ports without consent of the English producers ; even if electricity should take the place of steam, it must be many years before the coal demand will cease ; and to-day,

of the thirty-six millions of tons of coal required by
the steamers of the world, three-fourths of it is obtained from Great Britain.

It is unnecessary to wire-draw statistics, but it may,
as a last word, be interesting to show, with all our
development, the nationality and increase of tonnage
entering our ports since 1856.

Country.	Increase.	Decrease.
England............................	6,967,173	......
Germany	922,903	......
Norway and Sweden	1,214,008	......
Italy..............................	596,907	......
France............................	208,412	......
Spain	164,683	......
Austria...........................	204,872	......
Belgium...........................	226,277	......
Russia	104,009	......
United States	......	65,901

"This," writes Lindsay, "is surely not decadence,
but defeat in a far nobler conflict than in the wars
for maritime supremacy between Rome and Car-
thage, consisting, as it did, in the struggle between
the genius, scientific skill, and industry of the people of two great nations."

NOTE.—A comparative statement of the exports of grain from
this port to Europe in 1883 shows that the American steamer is no
longer on the ocean in the transatlantic trade, and that the American sailing vessel is there, so to speak, simply in name. Of the
1,190 steam vessels which last year crossed the ocean, carrying
44,205,009 bushels of grain, the United States cannot lay claim to
a single one ; while among the 166 sailing vessels, carrying 4,252,-
936 bushels, American ship owners are represented by two of the
very smallest cargoes, aggregating 25,650 bushels.

Of all the nations America is now the last, though in 1880 there
were seven nationalities—the Dutch, French, Danish, Portuguese,

Russian, Spanish, and Swedish—which were behind this country in the ocean carrying trade. Great Britain now heads the list in shipments by steamer, her record for the year being 786 vessels and 29,444,951 bushels, while Austria comes first in sailing vessels with a record of 51 vessels and of 1,498,684 bushels. Great Britain stands fifth on the list in shipments by sail, but by steam she carried 15,000,000 bushels more than all other nationalities combined.

It appears at a glance, that the sailing vessel is fast disappearing before the ocean steamer in the transatlantic carrying trade :

Year.	Steamers.	Sailing Vessels.
1879	1,056	1,798
1880	1,292	1,789
1881	1,302	554
1882	1,069	240
1883	1,190	166

Belgium has ceased altogether to be represented by sail, but she has pushed her way up to second on the list, not in the number of her carrying steamers, but in the bushels of grain carried.

The following table shows the shipments by steamer, and number of vessels and their nationality, which left this port in 1883 :

Nation.	No. of Vessels.	Bushels.
British	786	29,444,951
Belgian	93	5,734,018
German	170	4,248,485
Dutch	52	1,587,762
French	45	1,532,093
Danish	28	1,094,435
Italian	14	474,078
Portuguese	1	54,187
Spanish	1	35,000
Totals	1,190	44,205,009

Of this total there was in wheat, 17,448,747 bushels ; in corn, 22,125,678 bushels, and in rye, 4,636,523 bushels.

In the following table is shown the shipments by sail for the year :

Nation.	No. of Vessels.	Bushels.
Austrian..	51	1,493,684
Italian	47	1,230,690
Norwegian....	24	650,594
Portuguese....	17	352,560
British	11	259,091
Spanish	5	68,984
Swedish	3	50,443
Danish	2	42,947
German	2	41,533
Russian	2	31,760
American.....	2	25,650
Totals.......	166	4,252,966

Of this total there were in wheat, 3,495,728 bushels; in corn, 751,269, and in rye, 5,939 bushels.

The following shows the comparative shipments of grain by steamers and sailing vessels in the past four years :

Year.	Steam. Bushels.	Sail. Bushels.	Totals. Bushels.
1880........	49,966,579	63,376,584	113,343,163
1881........	53,255,728	19,020,583	72,276,312
1882........	39,878,449	6,284,289	46,162,738
1883........	44,205,009	4,252,936	48,457,945

CHAPTER III.

PUBLICISTS differ both as to the causes and the remedies. In 1865 the first were oracularly referred to
the war between the States; but in modern times
the effects of war are generally less potent when the
exciting cause is removed, and with us nearly every
other industry has quadrupled. At the close of the
Crimean war, Russian commerce was said to have
been destroyed, but with a favoring environment in
the four years subsequent to the peace, the damage
was so repaired that in 1860 48 per cent. more Russian ships entered English ports than ever before.

In 1868 doctrinaires declared that the fluctuation
of the currency was the destroying factor, but it is
of record that our shipping declined more after the
resumption of specie payments than in the years
when the fluctuations were greatest. Next followed
the assertion that with the revival of general prosperity so many avenues were opened to profitable
investment that no room was left for placing money
in the carrying trade ; but money has become cheaper
year by year, until now, with our shipping at low-
water mark, the rate is but 4 per cent., and for government bonds (excepting the consols of 1907) practically lower. None of these is a fair reason, for as
a matter of history the first actual decline began

before the war, in a time of fair interest and no
debts, and when money was stable. Some writers
assign it to various fanciful causes, and there are not
wanting others who discover the secret in British
gold, aided and abetted by an unholy trinity of
American venality, a hireling press, and a great foreign insurance combination. But it requires little
research to learn that the decadence must be as-
cribed to one or more of the following causes: 1.
Substitution of steam for sails. 2. Use of iron instead of wood in shipbuilding. 3. Non-subsidizing
of American lines. 4. Navigation Laws. 5. Special
Government and State restrictions.

In this country steam was first applied to the
navigation of rivers, and in 1847 the steam-tonnage
of the Mississippi Valley alone exceeded that of the
whole British Empire ; indeed, so great are the demands of our inland navigation that to-day it is
claimed our total domestic steam-tonnage does exceed that of England. By 1840 serviceable lines of
boats were plying between the principal commercial
cities of the Atlantic seaboard, and between 1845 and
1851 American steamers were crossing the Atlantic
ocean. In 1858 we had 52 steamers of 71,000 tons
in the foreign and domestic trades, England at
the same time owning 156 vessels of 210,000 tons
burden, and the rest of Europe 130 of 150,000 tons.
But in that year American competition broke down ;
and while we were left with only seven steam vessels
in the foreign trade, England had 120 plying to the
extremities of the earth. To-day foreigners have
over three hundred steamers in the direct trade with
the United States, while our country has less than

fifteen steamers running across the Atlantic and Pacific oceans.

Shipping cannot be measured merely by gross tonnage, for steamers, as determined by Leroy-Beaulieu, multiply the carrying power fivefold. They are cheaper than sailing vessels, as the birth-rate, death-rate and increase—"the vital statistics "—demonstrate. The ordinary life of a ship, allowing for extraordinary contingencies is, in the United States, 18 years ; in France, 20 ; in Holland, 25 ; in Germany, 25 ; in Great Britain, 26 ; in Italy, 28 ; and in Norway, 30. The annual average of wrecks for the seven years ending 1879 is as follows :

Country.	Steamers. Per cent.	Sailing Vessels.
British	2.94	3.93
French...................	2.47	4.04
United States.............	4.06	5.45
Dutch....	3.84	4.49
German	2.77	4.04
Italian...................	1.74	2.94
Scandinavian.............	1.96	3.20

Allowing three voyages yearly for a sailing ship and fifteen for a steamer, it appears that the former is lost once in 72 voyages and the latter once in 490 ; so that steamers have only one-seventh of the risk of sailing vessels. The death-rate of the world's shipping is 4 per cent., or 750,000 nominal tons, and the birth-rate 5 per cent., the average of new vessels built being 950,000 tons ; but even this does not give a correct idea, since the substitution of steamers for sailing vessels augments the carrying power 4 per cent. The vessels lost or broken represent 1,200,000 tons a year; and those built attain nearly double that number, as appears from Kaier's returns of the average since 1872, viz. :

Shipbuilding. Annual Average.

Dock Yards.	Steamers, Tons.	Sailing Vessels.	Carrying Power.
British..............	292,000	167,000	1,630,000
United States	15,000	118,000	193,000
Italy, Canada	35,000	324,000	499,000
	342,000	609,000	3,322,000

The efficiency of seamen measured by the number of tons they carry yearly will be found to have some relation to the quantity of merchandise borne by steamers, viz.:

Flag.	Seamen.	Tons Carried.	Per Seaman.	Steam Ratio. Per cent.
British	141,440	61,100,000	436	76
French......	29,220	8,100,000	271	63
German	39,980	5,700,000	141	54
Italian	52,000	4,300,000	83	25
Various	446,000	38,000,000	85	41
	708,640	117,200,000	165	61

Ten years ago the average of tons carried by each British seaman was no more than 278, so that two men in 1880 did the work of three men in 1870 ; and further, ships are not sent to sea short-handed, as this might indicate, for the efficiency of the seaman has been indisputably increased ; and the sea mortality of 3½ per 1,000 proves how much sanitary progress has gone hand-in-hand with the new conditions which demand superior intelligence. Some shipowners claim that owing to this very efficiency the car-

rying trade is overdone, and that the world could
satisfy its commercial demands with fewer vessels;
and though it is true that the ballast entries in Great
Britain and the Continent arose from $17\frac{1}{2}$ and $21\frac{1}{4}$
per cent. in 1870 to $19\frac{1}{2}$ and $22\frac{1}{4}$ per cent. respectively in 1880, still the building and employment of
new ships disprove this statement.   Tonnage movement, therefore, gives a better idea of national
wealth than tonnage possession, for the tendency of
trade is to transact business with that minimum of
profit and that maximum of volume which render
capacity and speed development essential. Twenty
years since a vessel of 3,000 tons on a voyage of
given length had to allow 2,200 tons for coal and
machinery ; but compound engines and structural
and propulsion improvements have so reversed this
that now but 800 space-tons are needed for motive
power, and 2,200 may be devoted to freight and passengers.   In 1883 Great Britain built five steamers
to each sailing vessel constructed ; and though a fair
proportion of the world's commerce is still carried in
sailing vessels, these figures seem to prove that, except for very long voyages with bulky freights, their
days are numbered.

But even in sailing vessels iron ships are super-
seding wooden, and during the last five years, while
we built 101,823 tons almost entirely for domestic
trade, England put afloat 1,800,193 tons ; and to-day
still further complicates the problem by proposing
the substitution of steel for iron.'

---

[1] " A recent English writer, in treating of the new application of
steel to shipbuilding, illustrates the advantage of this material over

In every important respect iron ships are more desirable than wooden : 1. They secure a higher classification and for a longer term of years ; 2. They are maintained at less expense ; 3. They carry more cargo on equal tonnage and obtain higher rates of freight ; 4. They command the preference at the enhanced rates ; 5. They are insured on better terms ; and, 6. They are less liable to damage cargoes.

All parties will accept these as primary causes of the decay of our shipping, their practical influences being coeval with the evolution of new theories of commerce ; but beyond these points of agreement there are two radical and embittered differences of belief, one pinning its faith to the dogma of free ships, and the other looking toward the Mecca of subsidies.

---

iron as follows ; Suppose the construction of a transatlantic freight steamer carrying 3,500 tons (dead weight) is contemplated ; if of iron, the hull will weigh about 2,500 tons, and the entire ship will cost about $350,000 ; if of steel, the hull will weigh 2,000 tons, the total cost being $380,000. Reckoning 6 per cent. interest and 6 per cent. depreciation, etc., on this $30,000 extra cost, we have $3,600 per annum. As an offset to this, the writer estimates as an extra freight on the steel over the iron vessel 500 tons cargo out and 500 tons cargo back. Assuming ten trips per year, this would give 10,000 tons extra freight, which, at $3 average freight per ton, would make $30,000 extra earnings per year. Deducting from this the $3,600, the balance of $26,400 represents the extra net profit per year that would be earned by the steel over the iron steamship, which is equal to 9½ per cent. on the entire cost of the vessel."

CHAPTER IV.

THE protection or subsidization of the American foreign trade is not a new idea in our experiments with political economy, the first appropriation dating from 1845, when $1,274,600 were *equitably divided* between several lines of steamers ; under varying conditions and with increasing demands these bounties were continued until 1855, and then ceased, not to appear until 1865, when Congress subsidized Garrison's Line to Brazil, and, later, the Pacific Mail and Roach's Brazil Line. To develop commerce for the ships we could build was offered as the apology for the subventions in the earlier period ; to foster shipbuilding as the most important element of commerce revival is claimed as their *raison d'être* in the latter. But herein lies a fallacy ; for while shipbuilding is of the navigation interests, it is not its rounded summation : commerce, carrying trade, postal service, and the maintenance of a school for maritime defence, being, if not superior, at least not subordinate. The profit of a ship in twenty years' cargo-carrying is fifteen times greater than her first cost, and, low as is our commerce to-day, more wages are distributed to sailors in a single week than all the shipbuilders pay their operatives in an entire year ; hence, it is a curious study in political economy to find an illogical conclusion resulting in national interests being sacrificed to the policy of a few ship-builders, and to see a great country rejecting a greater profit for a lesser because both cannot be obtained. "There is a familiar doctrine found in the Constitution of the United States and in the Constitution of every State," said Mr. Bayard in the Senate, "which is the necessary outgrowth of the in-stitution of government itself. It is that the interest of the individual or few must give way to that of society at large. But where is the proposition, and where in any civilized government called free can you find the doctrine recognized, that public prop-erty may be taken for private use?" It is undeni-able that under whatever form subsidies appear they tax the many for the few, and can be met only by new burdens upon the producer and consumer for the benefit of a privileged distributing agent; this protection means that the greater number of Ameri-can shipowners must compete not only with foreign and home rivals, but with their own more favored countrymen who sit above the salt and receive ex-ceptional favors from the Government; nay, more, it results in the nation itself entering into competition with the great body of shipowners and shipbuilders, whose contributions to the revenues are turned against themselves. When Congress compensates steamship lines for running at a loss, or pays the difference between the cost of running and what the owners consider a fair profit on their investment, the subsidized lines alone are profited, and the un-protected but restricted ships succumb in the unequal conflict. In nearly every case protected lines in the past have been beaten by unsubsidized but unrestricted foreign steamers ; when the bounties ceased the lines stopped running, and while freights were not made cheaper, the results were to make the protected owners richer by the subsidy, to ruin the unprotected shipper, and to develop no foreign trade. During the ten years covered by Garrison's operations the value of our imports from Brazil doubled, and our exports increased but one-eighth, and for this solution of the economic question we paid $1,500,000.

"Whenever the question of ships is raised, the clamor for subsidies and bounties is renewed, and we are told again that England has established her commerce by subsidies. . . . Some of our writers and speakers seem to be under a fascination which impels them to accept as authoritative examples the follies of English history, and to reject its sound lessons. In the present case, however, the matter stands somewhat differently. England is a great manufacturing town. It imports food and raw materials and exports finished products. It has therefore a general and a public interest in maintaining communication with all parts of the world. . . . Subsidies to ships for the mere sake of having ships or ocean traffic, when there was no business occasion for the subsidized lines, would have no analogy with English subsidies " (Sumner). Yet the example of Great Britain is invariably hailed as the clear, effulgent light whereby we may guide our stumbling footsteps, and we are asked to subscribe a few millions that we may replace England as a successful wooer for the commerce of the world. But even if our national conditions were as alike as they are dissimilar, an addition of 100,000 tuns to our ocean tonnage, supported by a bonus of $3,500,000, would be only 5 per cent. of the steam fleet of Great Britain, and its total earnings would be but 2½ per cent. of the freight money she bids us stand and deliver on the high seas. England is a country whose greatness is in dependencies which punctuate the page of the world ; 200,000,000 of her people demand postal communications in colonies separated by leagues of sea, and her sea-concessions are analogous to what we have done in railroad-grants and mail-routes within our undivided territory. Of the £783,000 voted in 1881, more than one-half went for mail purposes, and not a guinea was tabooed to ships surveying mankind with commercial view, or built in any country from China to Peru ; some of this bounty has gone to foreign ships under foreign flags, and her object has been, not to make Englishmen buy or build ships, but to force the colonies to recognize their indebtedness to the mother-country. France exports a good share of her manufactured goods in English-built ships, and Italy must necessarily do the same, as she has few others. Hence it seems certain, that for whatever reasons of policy and by whatever country this money is given, it is under no limitations to employ home-built ships or to foster home shipbuilding interests.

Our coasting trade, which includes the rivers and great lakes, now comprises about 19,000 vessels and 2,200 barges, employing 70,000 men, and the competition is so great that the charges for transportation have been reduced to a point never before known. Hence no one prominently identified with this question seeks to alter in the least the conditions of this enormous industry. It is true that there are a few dissatisfied writers who demand entire and immediate freedom for ships and tariff, but the great majority of free-ship advocates do not seek such extreme measures of relief; they do not wish, for instance, to interfere with this domestic trade, believing that its monopoly of 60 per cent. of the whole ship-building, and that the restrictions in the size of the vessels to be bought in open market (nothing under 3,000 tons for foreign trade), ought, with the revenues accruing from repairs, to double the income of shipbuilders, who will be carrying to a full development a reviving industry. For years these shipbuilders have been protected, and each year fewer ships have been built ; subsidies have been tried, but commerce still languishes ; the echoes of a world treating the great problem of supply and demand upon new principles have been heard and are unheeded ; and therefore is it that many men believe that a remedy exists, first, in the repeal of the navigation laws, and, secondly, in the removal of those other restrictions which have helped to throttle the fairest promise of modern days.

These navigation laws, so often quoted and so little understood that few of the laity can distinguish accurately between enrolment and register, and the best legal talent has been at fault in correctly defining the proper way of transferring the license of a pleasure-yacht from one collection district of the United States to another, can be found under title 48 of the Revised Statutes, Regulations of Commerce, chapters one to nine, and in various

scattered sections of the law and of the Treasury
Regulations. After our establishment as a nation,
the questions of Slavery, Trade, and States Rights
were the great sectional issues, and our Constitution
and the earliest statute laws were, to a large extent,
the results of compromises between these antagonistic ideas; indeed, that admired clause which provides no religious test shall ever be required as a
qualification for office, as well as the first amendment,
which forbids the establishment of religion or the
prohibition of its free exercise, were merely parts
of a general political necessity, restricting the functions of the federal government, and leaving to the
several States as much of their separate sovereignty
as was consistent with the existence of the Union.
A larger belief in the rights of conscience did not
engender this liberality, and the reasons of policy
which forbade the federal government to meddle
with Slavery applied with tenfold power to questions
of religion. So was it with the navigation laws, for
they originated in a compromise between the slave-
supplying and the slave-holding sections of the country; and the power to regulate commerce was in-
serted with, and, as a consideration for the extension,
by New England votes, of the slave-trade until 1808,
and for the prohibition of export duties. Though the
Middle States and Virginia and Maryland protested
against the infamous bargain, New England demanded from the first federal Congress assembled
under the Constitution her share of the disreputable
compact; and thus, conceived in iniquity and reared
in sin, the present navigation laws have cursed our
generations with more than Biblical prophecy. It is

but fair to add that their final enactment was in re-
taliation of the illiberal policy by which England
instituted the destruction of our trade with the
West Indies ; our triumph galled the British jade,
and wincing, she did not look placidly upon our un-
wrung withers. Pitt, with a small following, did attempt to liberalize trade upon the high seas, though
Lord Sheffield, who, among others, was in 1783 bla-
tant in two-penny opposition, advised the government to deal gently with the erring corsairs of
Barbary, as the operations of these discriminating
cut-throats would be confined mainly to the destruction of the commerce of America and that of the
weaker Italian states. Others preached a fine philanthropy, publicly entreating the British lion and the
American lamb to lie down together in peace, and
privately praying that the lamb might be inside of
the lion.

Somewhat curtailed, the navigation laws may be
summarized as follows : No American is allowed to
import a foreign-built vessel in the sense of purchasing, acquiring a registry, or using her as his property ; the only other imports, equally and forcibly
prohibited, being counterfeit money and obscene
goods. An American vessel ceases to be such if
owned in the smallest degree by a naturalized citizen, who may, after acquiring the purchase, reside
for more than one year in his native country, or for
more than two years in any other foreign state. An
American ship owned in part or in full by an American citizen who, without the expectation of relinquishing his citizenship, resides in any foreign country except as United States Consul, or as agent or

partner in an exclusively American mercantile house,
loses its register and its right to protection. A citizen obtaining a register for an American vessel must
make oath that no foreigner is directly or indirectly
interested in the profits thereof, whether as commander, officer, or owner. Foreign capital may build
our railroads, work our mines, insure our property,
and buy our bonds, but a single dollar invested in
American ships so taints as to render it unworthy of
the benefit of our laws. No foreign-built vessel can,
under penalty of confiscation, enter our ports and
then sail to another domestic port with any new cargo,
or with any part of an original cargo, which has once
been unladen previously, without touching at some
port of some foreign country. This law is construed
to include all direct traffic between the Atlantic and
Pacific ports of the United States *via* Cape Horn,
the Cape of Good Hope, or the Isthmus of Panama ;
and being a coasting trade, foreigners cannot compete. An American vessel once sold or transferred
to a foreigner, can never again become American
property, even if the transaction has been the result
of capture and condemnation by a foreign power in
time of war. Vessels under 30 tons cannot be used
to import anything at any seaboard town. Cargoes
from the eastward of the Cape of Good Hope are
subject to a duty of 10 per cent. in addition to the
direct importation duties. American vessels repaired
in foreign ports must pay a duty on the repairs
equal to one-half the cost of the foreign work or
material, or pay 50 per cent. *ad valorem*, the master
or owner making entry of such repairs as imports.
This liberal provision, which, dates from 1866, is

made to include boats obtained at sea, from a passing foreign vessel, in order to assure the safety of our own seamen. No part of the proper equipment of a foreign vessel is liable to duty, except it be considered redundant ; thus when two sets of chains were found upon such a vessel, one was made chargeable with duty. Foreign vessels arriving here in distress, with loss of equipment, must pay duties on the articles imported for repair ; if they need sheathing, 45 per cent. is exacted for the new copper used, and 4 per cent. for the old copper removed. In one case a foreign vessel left her mooring chains of foreign manufacture on an American wharf, and with great alacrity duties were immediately and lawfully collected on them as importations. If a citizen buys a vessel of foreign build stranded on our coast, takes her into port, repairs and renders her serviceable, she cannot become American property unless the repairs amount to 75 per cent. of the whole value of the vessel. Except in the fisheries, all our vessels engaged in foreign trade must pay annually a tax of 30 cents a ton ; a ship of 1,000 tons, for instance, contributing $300, which represents the profit and interest of $5,000 at 6 per cent. Vessels belonging to foreign states having commercial treaties with us pay the same tonnage dues ; but if an alien becomes an owner, even to a fractional amount, in an American ship, not only does the latter lose her registry, but the foreign privilege is void, and the joint ownership is charged with a tax of sixty cents a ton. If a picnic party comes into an American port in a foreign vessel—on the great lakes, for example, in a Canadian steamboat—such vessel becomes liable to

a tonnage tax. Though the act of 1872 made free
all material necessary for the construction of ships in
this country for foreign trade, such vessels cannot
engage in domestic trade for more than two months
in any one year without payment of the duties, for
which a rebate was allowed. Canal-boats crossing
the Hudson River, or any other navigable stream, are
making a coasting voyage, and must be enrolled and
licensed as coasters; in default of such precautions
they have been seized, and released only after much
delay and upon the payment of a fine. A foreign
private yacht, touching at different parts of our lake
or sea-coast, and carrying passengers—members of
other hospitable clubs—can be punished for violating the laws of domestic trade.

Such, briefly sketched, are some of the laws under
which a free people live, and for their repeal the
historic bill, No. 724, was introduced by Senator
Beck on January 27, 1880. Stripped of its official
verbiage, this proposed measure enacted that certain
provisions of the statute law be repealed, and that
hereafter it should be lawful for our citizens to purchase ships built in whole or in part in any foreign
country, and to have them registered as, and accorded the privileges of, ships built wholly within
the United States, and owned and controlled by our
citizens. It being a debatable question whether the
full measure of relief could be proposed anywhere
save in the House, under its power to originate
money or revenue bills, all provisions relative to
tonnage dues, local taxation, bonded ship stores,
and free material for construction and repair, were
purposely omitted.

Other evil agencies are at work, and the repeal of such of the laws as apply to foreign trade is only the first step ; prominent among these are consular fees, compulsory pilotage, State and local taxation, personal liability, determination of tonnage capacity, shipping, discharge and transportation of sailors, and protective duties upon shipbuilding materials. The limits of this argument forbid any but the following brief hints : For the year ending June, 1880, the Treasury received, mainly from American ships, $592,161 ; these fees, the interest of $10,000,000, being extorted in order that the consular service might be self-supporting, and not, as in England, maintained by the nation. Pilotage to New York is more than double that to Liverpool, and with a thorough appreciation of the energy, skill, and sacrifices of our pilots, it seems somewhat wrong that the Sandy Hook service, composed of one hundred and thirty-three New York and fifty-eight New Jersey members, should have received last year between $800,-000 and $1,000,000, or a mean average of over $5,000.[1]

---

[1] "The committee declared the pilot service a monopoly. The pilot fees are fixed by law, and can only be changed by act of the Legislature ; they were increased in 1865, in consequence of the gold premium, about 50 per cent., with an understanding, had with the merchants, that it should be for three years only, but this three-year clause was subsequently stricken out of the bill by act of the Legislature, and the fees have since remained as follows (the rates fixed by the act of 1853 and prevailing till 1865 being added for comparison) :

	Inward. Per Foot.	Outward. Per Foot.
For every vessel drawing less than 14 feet...	$3 70	$2 70
For every vessel drawing 14 feet and less than 18 feet.....	4 50	3 10
For every vessel drawing 18 feet and less than 21 feet.....	5 50	4 10
For every vessel drawing 21 feet and upward............	6 50	4 75

If compulsory pilotage be necessary—and this just men deny—how can the smaller merchant thrive under a system which makes it as expensive to bring a vessel into our harbors as it does to pay her captain for a round voyage to the West Indian ports ? In this country ships are assessed as personal property, in New York at a 60 per cent. valuation. The annual profits of a steamship costing $500,000 may be assumed to be $25,000, and her taxes in New York, at a 2½ per cent. rate on $300,-000, will amount to $7,500, or 30 per cent. of the average profit; in England the income of the ship alone is taxed, about $500 will satisfy the government's demands, and the ownership of a vessel which is idle or unprofitable does not entail those

---

"If a vessel be moored within Sandy Hook or detained at Quarantine, the pilot is entitled to his discharge and to full pilotage fees. When boarding a vessel beyond the sight of Sandy Hook Lighthouse the pilot is by law entitled to charge 25 per cent. in addition to the regular fee. This 'off-shore pilotage,' however, has been declared illegal by judicial decision, and is no longer collected unless specially agreed to by the master of the vessel. Between the first day of November and the first day of April $4 is added to the pilotage of every vessel coming in or going out of port.

"The committee presented a statement showing fees paid at several of the leading European ports, none of which are as easy of access as the port of New York. A ship drawing 21 feet in and 23 feet out has to pay for pilotage in and out at the port of Liverpool, $67.44 ; London, $147.55 ; Bristol, $125 ; Bremen, in summer, $55.85 ; Bremen, in winter, $88.79 ; New York, in summer, $245.75 ; New York, in winter, $253.75. The Sandy Hook pilot service comprises 22 boats belonging to the State of New York and 7 belonging to the State of New Jersey, the 29 having an estimated value of $300,000."—*From Report of Special Committee Chamber of Commerce, New York City.*

burdens which must weigh upon vessels assessed and
taxed under the same conditions as real estate. According to the British mercantile rule, the tonnage
capacity of vessels is measured only on cargo space,
allowance being made for quarters and machinery ;
with us the space occupied by the galley and closets
was until last year alone excepted, and as a consequence our ships suffered, not only at home, but in
·ports where harbor duties and light-money are levied.
Sailors discharged in foreign ports receive three
months' pay regardless of character or of the fact
that most of them are foreigners, and many of them
beach-combers, who double their wages by such
tricks, and that all of them are at home in any part
of the world.

Thirty-odd years ago the commerce of the world
was carried in sailing vessels, and it was no idle
boast when Americans claimed that England was
lagging in the great ocean race, because of our superior build and management of vessels. In many
important trades our magnificent clippers were the
favorite ships, and the great commercial interests of
England were so involved from the want of similar
vessels that remedial measures became necessary.
But England was shackled by navigation laws, the
first dating from 1380, and, strangely enough, offering as a panacea for existing evils "that no subject
of the king should ship any merchandise, outward
or homeward, save in a ship of the king's allegiance,
on a penalty of forfeiture of vessel and cargo."
Since Cromwell's time offensive prohibitions, not
unlike our own, had existed on her statute books,
broadening down from age to age by that precedent

so dear to the English heart ; and in 1849, when the
reform was finally debated, such men as Disraeli,
Brougham, and Bentinck declared that free trade in
shipping would ruin shipowners, drive the British
sailor into prospering Yankee ships, and destroy the
shipbuilding interests of Great Britain. Brougham,
skilled in brilliant misinformation, avowed that the
navigation law was not only the corner-stone of
England's glory, but the foundation of her very existence ; and Mr. Disraeli closed his protest against
the expected arrival of the same old New Zealander
by airily promising that "he would not sing Rule
Britannia for fear of distressing Mr. Cobden, but he
did not think the House would desire Yankee Doo-
dle." Shipowners sold their vessels at ruinous rates,
forswore the sea, and implored Parliament to save
them ; but in vain the protests and petitions, for the
intelligence of the country was aroused on behalf of
its pocket, and by a good majority the cause of progress triumphed. Thirty years since England was
more free than this country is to-day, and when, in
1856, the restrictions upon her coasting trade were
removed, she was in a position that our most enthusiastic free-ship men do not hope for in the lustrums
yet to be. England's new policy paid, for from 1840
to 1879 her tonnage movement, that is, the entrances
and clearances of English ports, grew from 6,490,485
tons to 30,943,506 tons, or an increase of 476 per
cent.

CHAPTER V.

FREE SHIPS.

ALL other nations have the power of buying ships for foreign trade in the cheapest market, and the effort to protect our shipbuilders by the denial of this right forbids the return of commercial prosperity. In the coast trade, foreign interference can be excluded, but upon the high seas our rivals cannot be taxed; we labor under the disadvantages of traditionally higher wages and better rations; but the same skill which enabled us up to 1860, with well fed, well paid and more intelligent crews, to overcome these difficulties, will not desert us now. By treaty we grant to Germans trading in ships of any build every right allowed our citizens in American built ships. Norway and Sweden, under commercial treaties, claim every privilege conceded to the Germans; and as France and England are granted by law all concessions yielded to the most favored nations, we have practically given the maritime peoples the power to compete freely with free ships for a trade we deny our merchants. Under this dispensation our seaboard cities have become stations where foreigners may loot our producers; we survey, buoy, and police our harbors mainly for foreign guests; and our grand lighthouse system holds out to burn so that these sinners against our greatness may

return, unregenerated, unrepentant, and voracious
for more of our material advantages. This is an agricultural country, nine-tenths of our products for
export being no further advanced in manufacture
than hogs idealized into pork, and wheat transmuted
into flour, which, being as perishable as they are
beautiful, must go abroad. To the monopolists,
free ships or ships protected mean nothing ; but to
the farmer, transportation spells profit or loss, life
or death almost. Millions are annually appropriated for railways, canals, river and harbor improvements, simply to move crops which, arriving at the
seaboard, find a lame and impotent conclusion in
foreign ships, ruled by a combination of home railways and alien shipowners and insurance companies.
As a rule, competition eastward keeps down the
price, but a syndicate of railroad men, charitably
excited by our necessities, can tax the country millions of dollars by increasing freights a few cents a
bushel on wheat and a dollar a ton on other articles,
which find at the home ports, not three thousand
ship-captains bidding for cargoes, but a secret agreement like that of 1873, when the great transatlantic
lines pooled and bled the country of millions.

Free ships foster American interests, while the
other policy develops, and will develop, the material
greatness of other countries. There is no injustice
of indiscrimination in subjecting to a high rate of
duties commodities imported separately, while allowing the vessels composed of these articles to be imported free ; *for the former are thrown upon a protected
market where the burden can be distributed, and the latter
compete in open market with ships that are unrestricted.*

We will not buy the condemned ships of England, and it is fair to suppose that the same judgment in the employment of a means to an end will be exerted here as in any other path where every justly balanced and economic element must be considered.

This great national question bears a special meaning to the service, for no law is better defined than the correlation and interdependence of the mercantile and naval marines. Honest men differ honestly as to causes and to remedies, and the way is not always clear ; but fairly considered, it seems that in the generalization of free ships lies the answer to the great economic enigma ; its literature is open to all, and the examples of our past and the past of other nations are of history. Superiority in the carrying trade is not due to the facility with which steamers can be built, nor to any one of a half-dozen different elements ; the books of the shipbuilders of the Tyne and the Clyde show that they build vessels as readily for other nations as for their own ; and in explaining this, an English writer declares that if the Americans had ten years ago repealed their suicidal Navigation Law, and bought or built a steamer for every British steamer built on the Clyde, they would to-day be in some position to compete with England in the carrying trade, instead of having to deplore their present state of destitution. " The effects produced by changes in the conditions of an industry are inevitable, and cannot be avoided by legislation ; the only solution that gives, is to cause the loss to fall on some other set of people instead of on those directly interested. Again : it is evident that a country needing a protective tariff on iron and steel cannot expect to supply ships for ocean traffic at the low price of competing constructors in countries of no tariff. For the country which by hypothesis needs a protective tariff on iron and steel cannot produce these articles as cheaply as some other country. Its ships, however, must compete upon the ocean with those of the country which has cheap iron and steel. The former embody a larger capital than the latter, and they must be driven from the ocean. If then subsidies are given to protect the carrying trade when prosecuted in ships built of protected iron, the loss is transferred from the ship-owners to the people who pay taxes on shore. These taxes, however, add to the cost of production of all things produced in the country, and thereby lessen the power of the country to compete in foreign commerce. This lessens the amount of goods to be carried both out and in, lowers freights, throws ships out of use, checks the building of ships, and the whole series of legislative aids and encouragements must be begun over again, with a repetition and intensification of the same results" (Prof. Sumner).

The men who ask for free ships are not the reckless theorizers their adversaries claim, and what they ask can be best exhibited in the particularized items, submitted in a late memorial to Congress :

1. The admission to American register of all ships over 3,000 tons, subject to the same laws regarding ownership that now prevail.

2. The admission of all materials to be used in the construction and repair of vessels of over 3,000 tons duty free.

3. The adoption of new tonnage measurements, based on actual carrying capacity and excluding the space occupied by engines and boilers and accommodations for officers and crew.

4. Exemption from taxation, local and national, of all vessels engaged in the foreign trade for more than eight months of the year.

5. Permission for all American vessels in the foreign trade to take their stores and ship-chandlery out of bond duty free.

6. A general revision of the laws relating to seamen and to the consular service.

As already shown, the advocates of both the great theories of relief accept all these conditions, save the first and second, as absolutely necessary for the regeneration of our merchant marine ; nay, many go so far as to find the second so little a matter of dispute that the adverse views may be said to separate only upon the first. Taken generally, the demands as formulated are moderate, and fairly represent the *juste milieu*, the golden mean, that has been attained by concession through the belief that anything more radical would not, under our governmental theory of taxation and with the existing conditions of the industries themselves, be justifiable. By the proposed remedies an American is enabled to buy his ship in the best and cheapest market, and to place it under the protection of a flag that is in little danger of war from outside complications. At the same time, under the restrictions of ownership, no foreign power, Great Britain for example, whose safety-valve and temper-check are in her carrying trade, would be able in war to place

her navigation interests under our protection without relinquishing ownership ; and alarmists may
therefore be certain that she will not be able to resort to the well-known process of whitewashing—a
system of bills of sale with counter-mortgages—
while holding fast to our legitimate opportunities.

What is more, both by original constructions and
repairs, ship-building would, under the liberal plan
proposed, be stimulated, and not only would the
corps of skilled workmen be retained, but private
shops filled with eager apprentices must, of the necessities of the case, spring up wherever coal and
iron and deep water-fronts made shipbuilding feasible.

Other remedies have been suggested, and they
run the gamut of theory, from the wildest license of
Free Trade to the grimmest asceticism of Protection.
These admit only of the briefest notice.   One is a
change of policy with respect to international trade,
a revival of the law of 1817 which forbade any ship to
bring a cargo to the United States except from the
ports of the country to which it belonged. This
policy might result in profit with South America
and Asia, for those countries own few ships trading
to the United States, and we have commerce with
them ; but England and the other maritime nations
would doubtless respond by a like enactment, and
thus deprive our ships of nearly all the general trade
we have outside our own country. As this is a simple
question of what will pay best, this proposed relapse
into the practices of barbarism need not be considered here ; neither would it be germane to call it, in
this age of private enterprise, the employment of a

policy that characterized the idyllic days when every essay was seconded by the sanction and effort of paternal government; though as a matter of demonstrable fact it may be sufficient to affirm that we would lose much, and not even get the credit of being martyrs to progress.

Mr. Blaine solves the problem by bounties, for this purpose enacting a general law which ignores individuals and enforces a policy. His scheme provides that any man or company of men who will build in an American yard, with American material by American mechanics, a steamship of three thousand tons, and sail her from any port of the United States to any foreign port, he or they shall receive, for a monthly line a mail allowance of $25 per mile per annum for the sailing distance between the two ports; for a semimonthly line $45 per mile, and for a weekly line $75 per mile. Should the steamer exceed three thousand tons, a small advance on these rates might be allowed; if less, a corresponding reduction might be made, keeping three thousand as the average and standard. Other reformers propose a bounty to be given by the government to the shipbuilder so as to make the price of an American vessel the same as that of a foreign-bought, equally good but presumably cheaper, ship. This will be brought about positively by hard cash, negatively by discriminative duties. There are a few enthusiasts, generally socialists and foreigners, who will be satisfied with nothing less than both the immediate abolition of all duties—not even retaining a modest tariff on luxuries for revenue—and the opening of the coast and domestic trade to the world. And last of all, at the other

swing of the pendulum, there are kindred spirits
who would abolish seamen, ships, and seas, turning
the last, for the eternal and cloistered happiness of
America, into walls of fire that would ban the foreign commercial invader.

What is most wanted is action, action, action.
From the beginning of the war to this hour Congress has not passed a single act to uphold the foreign carrying trade, and during the same time it has
enacted ninety-two laws in aid of internal transportation, has given in public lands an acreage larger
than that of the original States, and has added
$70,000,000 in money. A thorough-going Congres-
sional investigation of the whole subject of our commerce, manufactures, and navigation would be of
great service in enabling merchants and the government to co-operate harmoniously and intelligently.
It would bring about a better understanding between the agricultural, industrial, and mercantile
classes, and, revealing the directions in which effort
should be expended, it would tend to give us what
we greatly lack and so much need, " *a national policy
with respect to navigation.*" Something should be done
to make the ocean mail service bring a fair return to
the carriers; as our theory is that postages shall be
rated so as merely to pay expenses, it does not seem
fair to an important and admirable service that the
$400,000 of receipts over expenditures for foreign
mails should be retained by the government for the
benefit of star routes that begin and end nowhere ;
other conditions being equal, give the mails to our
own lines, pay a fair price for their transportation,
and above all things release our ships at once from

the existing burdensome postal restrictions.[1] Rigid inspections of vessels should be imperative ; so that in the event of a change in the Registry laws, no vessel could be admitted to the benefit of our protection which would not be so well-found and serviceable as to entitle her to a high rating.

In Free Ships with the co-ordinate measures of relief is the only solution of the problem submitted for discussion and proof. As yet the popular voice is not hoarse from singing of anthems in favor of the policy, and in high places there is much contemptuous denial of its claims ; but an active and an able minority believes that the cause is just and worthy of fighting for, and that in the end success is certain to come. Sketching the repeal of the Corn Laws, Buckle writes : "Those who knew the facts opposed the laws ; those who were ignorant of the facts favored the laws. It was therefore clear that whenever the diffusion of knowledge reached a certain point

---

[1] The merchant vessels of the United States are compelled by law to carry all mail offered to their masters by post-office authorities here and by consuls abroad, and to accept such compensation as Congress directs. "The necessity of delivering the mails is frequently a source of delay and great expense to a ship . . . whose plans upon touching at some port for telegraphic advices from home may be changed by the owners. No matter what the trouble, the ship is compelled to deliver the mails assigned, or forfeit all the rights and privileges of a vessel of the United States." Stages and wagons receive an average of $28 per mile of route per annum ; coast and river steamers, $43.50 ; railroads, $131—the compensation to these last ranging all the way from $35 to $538, $897 and $1,155. Merchant vessels get only about $1 per mile per annum,— the American steamers from Philadelphia to Liverpool receiving, for instance, about 80 cents.

the laws must fall. . . . The opposition the reformers had to encounter was immense, and although
the principles of Free Trade had been established
for nearly a century by a chain of arguments as
solid as those on which the truth of mathematics is
based, they were to the last moment strenuously re-
sisted."

The instinct for our country's good through that
larger freedom and more equal justice for all men
which vivify this question, has had just such a past,
and is finding just such a present ; but to those who
watch, there are not wanting signs and portents of
an equal triumph for its future.

CHAPTER VI.

MARINE DISASTERS.—THE IMPORTANCE OF A THOROUGH
TRAINING FOR OFFICERS AND SEAMEN.

THERE is a growing interest throughout the country
in the revival of our merchant marine. In newspapers and legislative bodies there is apparent a larger
appreciation of the vitality of the question, and those
who have most persistently insisted upon the value
of the industry as an important factor in the problem of national wealth and happiness have never
been more hopeful that some relief would be granted
by Congress. Connected intimately with this measure there are other interests which must not be neglected, and it is the duty of the government to
anticipate the demands that will be made upon it.
Ships without effective crews cannot compete successfully in an age where commercial power is the
price of unceasing vigilance and economy ; and the
officers and men of our merchant vessels should in the
next decade be as much superior to the complements
of ships of any other nation as they were in those
glorious days of rivalry when American pluck and
skill almost wrested the commerce of the world from
England. At present we have few modern ships ;
there is no school afloat in which merchant sailors
can be trained, and the 60,000 seamen we had at the
beginning of the war have disappeared. Since 1856

the evolution and development of new theories of commerce make new demands upon the navigation interests, and yet without a home fleet to give this training in youth, nor examinations and other tests to make it obligatory in manhood, we are discussing the creation of a modern steam fleet, to command which there are few officers properly qualified either by training or experience. When it is remembered that an error of judgment or a want of information upon a simple matter may in some cases, nay, has in many, led to the sacrifice of hundreds of lives, or that a single shipwreck may represent $2,500,000, it becomes a question both with the government and with shipowners to find the best men capable for such enormous responsibility. On shore, where a thousand unforeseen circumstances do not complicate the question, a person intrusted with an enterprise of equal pecuniary magnitude would be required to furnish most crucial tests of his fitness for the business in hand ; and no company nor legislative body would be acquitted of blame which failed to take the precautions that promised reasonable security to invested capital and absolute safety to human life.

As yet our government has done almost nothing, though periodically some unhonored and unsung Plimsoll does attempt to improve the condition of the service and to ameliorate the hardships of a life which it does not need man's injustice or carelessness to make among the most rigorous in the human environment. It is true that the shipping of seamen is under control of government officers, but this is not, under the existing regulations, an unmixed blessing. For the steamboat service there is a rule of thumb inspection which is conducted by a star-chamber process, in a rough and ready kind of way ; and the Life Saving Service and Revenue Marine, with limited appropriations, are doing as good work as can be expected from the imperfect organizations which further personal interests and hamper general efficiency. Still, so far as any general law goes, or the possession of any new system regulating the conditions which perforce surround the control of merchant shipping, it may be safely asserted that none exists. Abroad the subject has received the closest attention, and to-day the efficiency of the British sailor is so much improved that where ten years since the average of tons carried by each seaman was only 278, now it is 436, or in a ratio of the labor of two men in 1883 equalling that of three in 1873. In our whole country there is but one ship in which the future merchantman is receiving preliminary training ; and, though the work of the St Mary's is most excellent, yet it seems absurd that out of $3,500,000 appropriated for education in the State the one hundred and twentieth part only should go to the schooling of the men who are to man and command the ships of the future. Still worse is it that a State should be compelled to burden its citizens with duties that belong to the people of a whole country ; and it would be farcical, were it not almost criminal, to find a population of 50,000,000 contributing each year about twenty-five trained American boys to a commerce which, notwithstanding its unparalleled decadence, is still the second in the world.

In 1880 the number of men employed in English merchant ships was 200,000—120,000 in sailing ves-

sels, and 80,000 in steamers—and of these the estimated annual waste reached the enormous figure of
16,000, 500 alone being officers ; to replace this loss
is a question that has received intelligent study and
action, yet with government aid and comfort and
the commissioning of eighteen training ships, two of
which are for officers, this annual waste is so illy replaced that England is compelled to man her ships
with foreigners to some considerable degree. The
first duty of a sailor is evidently to take care of his
ship ; to navigate her upon the high seas, and with
safety and certainty to make his ports of destination ;
yet to-day it is a matter of record that one-half of the
wrecks are due to preventable causes, and that in
England, for example, two-thirds of the wreckages
are set down by the British Board of Trade as the
results of ignorance and incompetency. If this be
true, and statistics prove it, under a system which
demands from masters and mates the possession of
certain elements of fitness for their duties it would
be natural to deduce that in a country where no
specially tested qualifications are required more disasters would occur ; otherwise education and training go for nothing. Then again, there should be
under the first system a relative annual decrease of
wreckages, for if this do not appear then the safe-
guards which the nations are giving each year to
navigation are useless, and in vain are the surveys,
lighthouse organizations, improved instruments of
navigation, steam lanes, charts, etc., which supple-
ment the diffusion of nautical science and the executive control over insurance corporations, ship owners and merchant masters and their assistants.

Certain writers have claimed that an analysis of
the files of the Bureau Veritas and of the English
wrecking list confirms the statement that, as the tonnage of the merchant marine increases each year, so
in like proportion do the disasters to vessels seem
to grow. Broadly tested this is not true ; for, apart
from every other reasonable consideration, it implies either that the same intelligence and the same
application of means to an end are not being employed in the science of navigation as in every other
economic question, or that the morality of seafaring
people in an age when the world is improving must
be retrograding. Professor Rogers finds, from his
comparisons and examination of trade statistics, that
in Great Britain there is an increase in the number
of wrecks and casualties, with a decrease in the.
number of vessels, this decrease for the years 1856–
1873 being 1 per cent. In the same period the increase of tonnage was 19 per cent. ; the increase in
the number of wrecks, including collisions, was 33
per cent. ; the increase in the number of collisions
was 23 per cent., and the increase in the number of
wrecks, excluding collisions, 36 per cent. Compar-
ing the number of collisions which occurred in
Great Britain with those of the United States, he
finds that the ratio of the former is as 1 to 67, and
that of the latter as 1 to 43 ; therefore, he argues,
since in a large number of cases the average of all
causes, except carelessness, which produces collisions must be a constant, the modulus of carelessness between the two countries may be stated to be
nearly at 2 to 3 in our favor. He finds further
that the proportion of wreckages, excluding colli-

sions, is somewhat less with us, though he admits
that the data of the Life Saving Service, except for
the past four years, is neither full nor reliable.
There is a wide discrepancy between these results
and those of Mulhall, who shows, upon an examination of Lloyd's Register, that between 1880 and the
preceding fourteen years there were in 1866–1879 an
average of 2,171 vessels lost, and in 1880 2,193, an
increase of but 1 per cent. ; while in the same period
the over-sea traffic had risen over 70 per cent. A
writer in the *Quarterly Review*, supposed by Brassey
in his book on British seamen to be Farrer, a master of statistics and of administrative and legislative
details, says for every ship lost in 1833–35 there were
3,794 tons on the register and 7,714 tons in foreign
trade ; while in 1870–72 there were 6,547 tons on the
register and 24,909 so employed. For every 100 tons
lost in 1833–35 the tons were respectively 2,656 and
5,401, and in 1870–72 the figures were 2,242 and 8,529.
For every life lost in 1833–35 there were 2,276 tons on
the register and 4,628 tons in the foreign trade, and
in 1870–72 the statistics give 3,635 and 13,831 tons.
Tabulating these figures they appear as follows :—

	Tons on Register.		Tons in Foreign Trade, United Kingdom.	
	1833-35.	1870-72.	1833-35.	1870-72.
For every ship lost.....	3,794	6,547	7,714	24,909
For every 100 tons lost.	2,656	2,242	5,401	8,529
For every life lost.....	2,276	3,663	4,628	13,831

The above results are so striking that he had them
tested in another way. The number of ships actually employed in the trade of the United Kingdom
being known from the year 1849, the number employed in the earlier years has been estimated from

them, and the wrecks at the different periods have been compared with these numbers, showing the average annual percentage of ships lost to average number of ships employed to be as follows :—

Periods.	Average.	Periods.	Average.
1833–35	3.72	1860–62	3.00
1841–42	3.20	1870–72	2.95

These figures dispose of the allegation that employment in British shipping is far more dangerous now than it was forty years ago, at a time antecedent to the repeal of the navigation laws.

Between 1866 and 1880 the steam tonnage increased from about 1,500,000 to 4,000,000 tons, and its carrying capacity from 40 to 61 per cent. as compared to a decrease in sail-carrying tonnage of from 60 to 39 per cent.

The relative national losses of vessels in the same period are shown by Kaier, an eminent Norwegian statistician, to have been :—

1879.	Steamers. Per Cent.	Sailing Vessels. Per Cent.	Total. Per Cent.
United States	4.06	5.45	9.51
Dutch	3.84	4.49	8.33
British	2.94	3.93	6.87
German	2.77	4.04	6.81
French	2.47	4.04	6.51
Scandinavian	1.96	3.20	5.16
Italian	1.74	2.94	4.68

This disproves the assertion so often made that the relative loss of steamers is greater than that of sailing vessels ; and it makes apparent that our loss is the greatest, a third more than England and double that of Italy, and that the fewest wrecks occur among Italian vessels, due probably to the fact

that in all long voyages increased care is secured because each sailor has a share in the ship. It will be
seen that Norwegians have, likewise, a very low percentage, which may arise from the preponderance of
sailors and ship-owners in that country ; for there is
almost a ton of shipping for each inhabitant, or five
times as much as the ratio in Great Britain. Allowing three voyages yearly for a sailing vessel and
fifteen for a steamer, the first is lost once in 72 voyages and the second once in 490 voyages, giving the
latter class but one seventh the risk of the former.
The ordinary life of a ship is, in the United States,
18 years ; in France, 20 years ; in Holland, 22 years ;
in Germany, 25 years ; in Great Britain, 26 years ;
in Italy, 28 years, and in Norway, 30 years. The
annual death-rate of the world's shipping is 4 per
cent., or about 750,000 tons, and the birth-rate 5 per
cent., or 950,000 tons of vessels built ; but since the
substitution of steamers for sailing vessels gives an
augmentation of 4 per cent. in carrying power the
loss is represented by 1,200,000 tons annually, and
the gain is about double, or 2,322,000 tons. During
1882, 198 steamers were lost, the nationality and
tonnage being as follows :—

Nation.	No.	Tonnage.	Nation.	No.	Tonnage.
British	141	151,041	American	15	11,568
French	6	6,486	Danish	6	3,274
German	5	4,562	Swedish	4	2,458
Spanish	4	4,177	Dutch	3	4,390
Belgian	3	4,643	Brazilian	3	4,643
Chilean	2	1,150	Various	8	4,425

Four of these steamers were built of steel, five of
wood, and the remainder of iron ; the largest pro-

portion of these losses was due to stranding, 99
being cast away by the ignorance, over-confidence
or carelessness of the people in charge ; 30 were lost.
by collision, 40 foundered, 7 were burned, 6 were
abandoned, 2 were sunk by ice, 1 broken in two, 1
exploded, and 11 were missing. Very few sailors
know the number of ships that have never been
heard from after leaving port, for in Great Britain
alone, in 1873–74, there were 80 vessels missing ; in
1874–75, 137, and in 1875–76, 101 ; between 1864–1869,
of 10,588 reported lost, the fates of 846 are unknown,
and even this frightful list is said to be less than
more accurate information or more extended insurance would show.   In 1877 the losses of the English
merchant marine comprised 560 sailing vessels
and 68 steamers, representing a value with cargoes
of $18,000,000 and of 2,700 lives ; and in 1875 the
total wrecks of all nationalities were 4,259, or a
number equal to that employed in our whole sea-
going service.   Appliances, however, for saving life
are becoming every year more effective, no less than
1,295 crews having been saved in 1880, as compared
with an average of 1,023 in the preceding years.
The number of persons drowned by shipwreck in
1880 was 1,725, and the average per annum since
1866 was 1,775, showing a decrease of 3 per cent.

A careful investigation of the causes of wreckage
shows many curious and unexpected results. Among
other general principles which have been deduced
is that over one-half the number of wrecks occur
when the wind blows less than a fresh gale, or
when a ship, if properly found, manned, and navigated, could keep the sea with safety.   From 1864

to 1874, inclusive, 229 vessels were wrecked during calm weather; 360, in light airs; 1,010, light breezes; 405, gentle breezes; 1,689, moderate breezes; 2,131, fresh breezes; 2,329, strong breezes; 919, moderate gales; 1,020, fresh gales; 4,320, strong gales; 1,921, whole gales; 373, storms; 666, hurricanes; 57, variable, and 639 unknown. The number of wrecks is proportionally larger for new vessels than for those that have reached the average age of service. Without giving the general table which may be found in the "Proceedings of the United States Naval Institute" (vol. vii. No. 3) and in Plimsoll's "Monograph on Seamen," the statistics show the age of greatest loss for England is between the twenty-first and thirtieth years of the ship's age— 3,418 being lost then as compared to 1,802 between the thirty-first and fortieth years; 2,747 were lost between the fifteenth and twentieth years, as compared to 3,111 between the third and seventh years.

Country and Period.	Ballast	Coal.	Fishing Smacks.	Grain, etc.	General Mdse.	Lumber.	Stone, etc.	All Others.	Total.
Mean Great Britain, 1864–74	235	623	126	146	93	98	143	621	2,210
Mean United States, 1875–79	447	259	81	99	120	267	36	629	1,938
Totals	682	882	207	245	213	365	179	1,250	4,148

For the United States the greatest loss is between the third and seventh years, 1,267 wrecks as compared to 875 between the fourteenth and twentieth

years, and 874 before the third year. To a large extent the number of wrecks is dependent on the character of the cargoes carried.

After making a liberal allowance for the larger
number of vessels engaged in certain kinds of trade,
it still remains proved that there is an excessive
number of wrecks corresponding to certain classes
of cargoes. Colliers are the most exposed to danger ;
next come ships in ballast, and then lumber vessels,
these last being indubitably caused by the venerable
age and decrepit character of the craft employed.
To become a " lumber drogher," as it is called, is the
sere and yellow leaf of a ship's existence, and as one
of these wallows across the Western Ocean or down
the North Seas it is the scoff and jest of every trim-
built clipper which shows a foaming wake and an
underwriter's rate that are the golden dreams of the
ocean tramp's skipper. With steamers grain and coal
are the most dangerous cargoes. The latter is apt to
cause loss by spontaneous combustion, caused by the
shipment of certain kinds of coal in a wet condition,
together with bad ventilation through the body of the
cargo. No extraordinary precautions are needed, but
ordinary care is not always given, whether from ignorance or carelessness, or from both, it is difficult to
say. This is more difficult to understand when an
effective tell-tale which gives warning of danger can
be made by inserting through the top of an ordinary thermometer a copper wire that will extend to
the 100 degrees line Fahrenheit, for example. This
wire is in electrical connection with a battery and
an alarm bell kept in any convenient spot. The moment the temperature of the heating coal expands

5

the mercury to the 100 degrees mark, the circuit is closed through the wire, battery, bell, and the return wire to the mercury bulb at the bottom of the thermometer, and a signal is rung continuously.

Grain cargoes are still improperly loaded in bulk, and are often stowed without shifting boards ; and there are not wanting underwriters who will insure such cargoes, often at values both of ship and freight which they know to be fictitious. For fraudulent insurance is a prolific cause of wrecks, and what is worse, in England, where those things are ordered differently, the remedy is not apparent. In our country we have insurance men who, for skill and probity, are unsurpassed in the world, and yet inquiry among them demonstrates the futility of hoping to eradicate this criminal practice. In 1867 there were in the Baltic 215 British vessels and 220 Swedish. The former had large insurances and the latter scarcely any, and of these 17 British vessels and 3 Swedish were lost. From 1857 to 1867 the ratio of loss was 10 British to 3 Swedish, and this difference cannot be accounted for by any superior skill of the north country navigator, and gives internal evidence of no relation to any underlying cause save the differences between the amounts of insurance.

Two sources of information are open to any one wishing to ascertain the ratio of wrecks and to deduce the causes :—First, the numerical data furnished by the Bureau Veritas of France, by the Wreck Register for Great Britain, and by the reports of the Life Saving Service of the United States. Secondly, the comparison of the findings of the courts of inquiry upon the causes of wrecks, casualties and collisions, ordered by the British Board of Trade or reported to this Board. By the Merchants' Shipping Act of 1854 it was assumed in the preliminary courts of inquiry that a vessel might be lost by any one of thirteen specified causes, the list beginning with the act of God, running through culpable inefficiency, and ending by the act of the Queen's enemies. At present the causes are relegated to four classes :—First, accidents, etc.; second, errors, ignorance, neglect, etc. ; third, defective material ; fourth, perils of the sea. From an examination of 15,828 English and 1,367 American casualties, it was found that for the total number of wrecks, excluding collisions, 45 per cent. was due to preventable causes, and in 1,267 trials by the officers of the British Board of Trade there were but 504 clear acquittals. Including with these the class of wrecks for which no cause can be safely assigned, that involving vessels which were never heard from after sailing, and those other wrecks for which it is exceedingly difficult to determine the true cause, the general conclusion is reached that about one-half of all the wrecks which occur are due to preventable causes. That is, ignorance or dishonesty is the fruitful source of an enormous loss of life and capital which could be saved.

The remedy for these, for both can be treated with some hope of cure, is in education. The lawmakers should be educated so as to frame a general law which will elevate and protect the merchant marine. In England the Merchants' Shipping Act has been productive of the greatest good, and, as has been shown, there is every year a steady decrease in the number of wrecks ; and as the tests for officers' certificates are increased there will be a like decrease in the causes now classed as preventable. With us especially, should a committee be intrusted with the duty of providing an organization, the duties of which will be analogous to those of the British Board of Trade ; and in place of one school-ship there should be a dozen, governed under the same general plan as the Naval Training Squadron, and turning out yearly, if not enough lads to supply the annual loss of American seamen, at least enough to fill the place of the officers, without whom we would be almost helpless in peace or war. We want good officers, not only for the protection of life and property, but also to secure for our seamen judicious and thorough commanders. Under the most stringent inspections, inefficiency upon the part of the master often leads to shipwreck, and it is only by enabling officers and men to learn their duties—professional and moral—and subjecting them periodically to tests and examinations, that we can be assured vital interests are not being sacrificed. Sailors are the pioneers of civilization and, with maritime countries, the reliance upon which the nation's honor and safety mainly depend.

CHAPTER VII.

An intelligent English officer declared, in a discussion upon the relative values of French and British naval training, that one suffered from too much system and the other from too little, and that English supremacy—which he claimed—was in spite, not in consequence either of national legislation or of public spirit. In these days, when trade is the active social principle, many radical changes have been introduced in commercial theories, and there is a wider appreciation of its demands and of the close relation existing between national and merchant marines. Abroad these changes have generally been in the direction of progress, but at home not only has there been retrogression, but an absence of that genius which, despite national neglect, should have triumphed over an unfavorable environment and placed us, at least, upon an equality with those smaller nations which of old we scorned as rivals. Our navy has been made ridiculous by insufficient appropriation, and the same criminal carelessness of Congress, acting in other channels, has nearly driven from the sea a merchant marine which five and twenty years since was the peer of England's in size and value, and the unchallenged superior of every other nation's in promise and efficiency. The country, however, seems awakening to the necessities of the sea-going trade, and our future is not without hope. What we should do to meet the demands to be made upon us is not always clear, but after thirty years' trial in other countries certain principles as points of departure may be said to have been established. Between the rigorous lines which the government in France lays down for the conduct of every enterprise and our own untrammelled liberty of neglect there must be a golden mean. Nowhere is there apparent a system so harmonious that every national condition can be satisfied, but there are evident, wherever any system does exist, the possibilities of a compromise between that executive control and that unhampered energy of the individual, which show in a tentative age like ours what a wiser generation may accomplish.

France, Italy, Great Britain, Russia, and the North Countries rejoice in a plan of some sort, but so far as our necessities demand, and to the degree that practice can justify theory, England of all the nations appears to have secured what we should essay. Not that her plan is perfect ; for wreckages, bad management, and criminal loss of life—all due to preventable causes—justify the demands for improvement which so many thinkers advance. Indeed, there are not wanting men of a wide experience in ship owning and ship governing who declare that, since the repeal of the navigation laws, eighty-nine per cent. of the British seamen has deteriorated professionally, sixty-five per cent. physically, and seventy-one per cent. morally. On the other hand, experts like Brassey, Lindsay, and Farrer deny this and affirm, upon what seem fair grounds of proof, that the sailor of our time is as competent as any seaman of the days of Drake or Nelson, and in every direction is more to be depended upon than in those years of long voyages, hard knocks, and scurvy. And as it is with the men so it is with the officers, for, without yielding a tithe of the admiration and respect which justly belongs to the mates and masters of the old clipper ships, it is undeniable that the demands made upon the modern merchant officer, where a modern marine exists, have resulted in the necessity for and the production of a superior man. This last is especially true in England, and, though something is attributable to the upward lift of all classes in the wave-sweep of progress, yet it is mainly due to the conditions which the British system imposes. France does well, but her best ships are commanded by naval officers, and her plan is based upon a theory which, however suited it may be to our necessities, is at variance with our national instincts. Its underlying principle is that every individual owes personal service to the State, either in the army or navy; and it is the natural outgrowth of that paternal rule which is the basis of every Gallic trial of government, be the theories of the rulers of the hour or accident what they may. For two hundred years the seafaring classes have accepted this, but it is certain we would dare neither to justify nor to put it in practice. One of its consequences is to give France to-day the best internal naval organization in the world. Under its perfection of detail a sailor may be transferred from a three-decker gunnery ship, manned by over a thousand men, to a corvette with a personnel of two hundred, and without changing the station number given him in the first ship, take up his duties and perform in the second proportionally the same amount of labor alow and aloft.

The merchant service is under equally rigorous control, and as every man in it must at some time have served in the national fleet, it is at all seasons a reserve from which trained men can be drawn in any emergency. The crews of the French navy are supplied from three sources—first from the *inscription maritime;* secondly, from voluntary enlistment, and thirdly, these methods failing, from conscription in the political departments touched by the tides. The greatest number belong to the first class ; in it is inscribed every one who has arrived at his eighteenth year and who has made two deep-sea voyages, either in a public or a private ship, or who has been for eighteen months in the coasting trade, or for two years in the home fisheries, and who in every case declares himself as wishing to continue a seafaring life. All persons in any way connected with the working of steam machinery afloat are likewise subject to this inscription, and are called into active service when the twentieth year is attained. The first period of obligatory service is for five years, three of which must be in actual service afloat ; but at any time, and especially during the fourth and fifth years, leave without pay may be granted to go to sea in any capacity, and should this leave be spent in the coasting trade, home fisheries, or on short voyages, the time is counted as if employed in the service of the State. Succeeding this first period there is another of two years, during which the *inscrit* is nearly always in the position of renewable leave. Certain advantages accrue for this service. Inscribed seafaring men alone have the right to follow that trade ; they are freed from the public service save in the navy and at marine arsenals during periods of necessity ; they can decline to have soldiers billeted upon them during their term of service and for four months after its expiration ; they are exempt from acting as guardians to minors ; they are admitted gratuitously to the hydrographic schools established for those who wish to prepare for the grade of officer, and they can travel while in service—that is, for seven years—on all railways at one-fourth rates. No person may command a merchant vessel unless he is twenty-four years of age and has passed sixty months at sea in actual service on board either a man-of-war or a merchant ship. His birth certificate, a record of his services, and a testimonial of good conduct, attested by the mayor of his place and *visé* by the commissioner of the *inscription maritime* of his arrondissement, must be produced, and, in addition, he must give evidence of his professional and intellectual attainment before a board of rigorous examiners. After twenty-five years seafaring, or after the fiftieth year has been reached, every one on the inscription list is entitled to a pension, whether he has done any actual service to the State or not. These particulars, which are taken from excellent reports by Lieutenant Commander Chadwick and Professor James Russell Soley, both of the United States Navy, make evident that this system is not adapted to the needs of our country, and during later political excitements in France sufficient protest has been awakened to show that, if the tradition and precedent of so many years did not sustain its claims, the system would be replaced by some other which would not so largely imperil personal freedom and so vigorously shackle individual energy. That its effects in certain directions have been good is unquestionable, but the characteristic fault of too much system is everywhere apparent. There is a sacrifice of results to methods, and efforts seem to be exerted which look rather to the perfection of the machinery than to the work done by the machine. It is the outcome of extreme centralization, though fortunately the evil effects reach more nearly the minor details than the larger plan, for, as in all such systems where the agents ally great personal ability with a willingness to sacrifice much but not all to the logical idea, sufficient elasticity has resulted to give a unity of purpose, a distinct perception of the ends proposed, and an adaptation of means to reach them. The wonderful organization, although dating from Colbert's time, was first revealed during the Crimean war, and showed how much France owed primarily to its great finance minister, then to Lalande and Hugon, and later to De Joinville, a prince of the blood, and one of the best sailors who ever walked a ship's deck.

England learned by actual comparison afloat both the low state of her seamen and her want of any system, and there were naval experts who grimly confessed that the next Trafalgar might have a Breton Nelson who flew a tricolor at his masthead and ran up signals that began and ended with *La France*.

Humiliating as the lesson might be it was made a wholesome one, and the results of intelligent study have enabled England to replace an annual waste of twenty-four hundred blue jackets with an equal number of trained apprentices, who, individually, are worth a dozen of the riff-raff formerly sold by the crimps at a guinea a head to the press gangs and recruiting officers. Nor has the merchant service been forgotten, and when we see a concrete and coherent system which tends to the continuous improvement of workingmen who should be placed upon the same basis as those of any other trade, we cannot but be alarmed for our future where effort may be wanting in the direction of necessary radical change. We have never had a definite plan in this country, the interests of owners being supposed sufficient to guarantee proper shipkeepers, and, trusting to this or to some other unhappy chance, we have silenced all mild protests and throttled all attempted energy by emphatic affirmations of the success of the good old days when we were the favorite commerce carriers.

It is evident that to maintain an efficient mercantile marine four conditions must exist : First, there must be a centralized system; secondly, effective ships; thirdly, good officers and crews ; and fourthly, an adequate reserve for supplying deficiencies in the personnel. No country has more fully recognized the importance of these correlated interests than Great Britain, and to-day the proof of her appreciation rests upon the incontrovertible fact that she is the leading maritime nation of the world.

The English system went into effect with the enactment, in 1854, of the Merchant Shipping Act. This was amended in 1855 and in 1862 ; and finally, in 1867, was given the form which it retains substantially to this day. In the "Manual" codified by a London publisher, the acts are arranged, according to subject-matter, under eleven heads :—First, The Board of Trade ; second, British Ships ; third, Masters and Owners ; fourth, Safety and Prevention of Accidents ; fifth, Pilotage ; sixth, Lighthouses ; seventh, Mercantile Marine Fund ; eighth, Wrecks ; ninth, Liability of Shipowners ; tenth, Legal Procedure, and eleventh, Miscellaneous—under this last chapter being included regulations for coolie contract labor, power of colonial legislatures to alter provisions of the act, etc. The enumeration of these eleven general divisions, with the variety and preciseness of details under each, gives evidence of the great labor and intelligence devoted to the question in England, and makes it, so far as breadth and particularity go, an unequalled code of maritime law.

The book is prefaced by a short chapter in which the short titles of the acts and the legal terms employed are briefly defined. Among these last Her Majesty's dominions are said to be the dominions so called and all territories either under the government of the East India Company or governed by any charter or license from the Crown or Parliament. A British possession is any colony, plantation, island, and settlement within the dominion and not within the United Kingdom. In all of these the Acts are operative under certain privileges accorded colonies, and to carry them out there is constituted a Board of Trade, which is defined to be "the Lords of the Committee of Privy Council, appointed for the consideration of matters relating to trade and foreign plantations."

To the Marine Department of this Board of Trade is entrusted the general superintendence of all matters relating to British Merchant Ships. Under the general heads enumerated above, the Board has direct or appellate control of the description and ownership of British vessels ; of the tonnage, measurement, and registry ; of the transfer and transmission of shares on ships ; of mortgages and sales ; and of forgeries and false declarations of ownership. Under the caption of Masters and Seamen is stated the authority which decides all questions affecting the personnel of the service. It regulates and establishes Local Marine Boards and Mercantile Marine Offices and the examinations and certifications of masters, mates, and engineers. It provides apprentices to sea service, and has control of the engagement of seamen, allotments and remittances of wages, savings-banks for seamen, legal claims to wages and mode of recovery on default of payment, relief to seamen's families out of the poor-rates, wages and effects of deceased seamen ; discharge of seamen abroad ; relief and return of distressed seamen ; volunteering into the naval service ; provisions, sanitary rules, and accommodations ; protection of seamen from imposition ; internal and general discipline ; naval courts relating to the merchant marine on the high seas and abroad ; registration and returns respecting seamen ; official logs ; unseaworthy ships ; greatest draught of water ; deck and load lines ; boats for sea-going ships ; ships' lights and fog-signals ; rule of the road at sea ; build, equipment, and survey of steamers ; misconduct of passengers on steamers ; inquiries into accidents, casualties, wrecks, and salvage ; general supervision of pilotage as established by local authorities, including the general regulations for pilot boats, licenses, signals, licenses for masters and mates, compulsory pilotage, and the rights, privileges, remuneration, and offences of all pilots ; and finally, of the mercantile marine fund. The management of light-houses, beacons, and buoys lies within the jurisdiction of special authorities for each of the three Kingdoms : the Trinity House for England, the Commissioners of the Northern Light for Scotland, and the Corporation of the Port of Dublin for Ireland. Under such specific regulations the seamen of Great Britain are trained, shipped, protected, and discharged under all possible contingencies. Of the various duties cited here only a few need further explanation.

Local Marine Boards are subordinate officers of administration established in seaports and other selected places to enforce the provisions of the law. These boards are made up of three classes—first, of the *ex officio* members, consisting of the mayor or provost and stipendiary magistrate of the place, or such of them as the Board of Trade selects ; secondly, of four members chosen by the same authority from persons residing in or having a place of business at or within six miles of the port ; and thirdly, of six other members elected for three years by the owners of ships registered in the port, every owner of not less than 250 tons having for every 250 tons one vote for each member, providing that no one individual's one shall exceed ten. This local board controls the maritime affairs of the district, establishes shipping offices now called mercantile marine offices, and appoints over each of these a superintendent. The duties of this officer are to afford facilities for engaging seamen by keeping registries of their names and characters ; to superintend their engagement and discharge ; to provide means for securing their presence on shipboard at the proper time and in proper condition, and to encourage and provide apprenticeships. In the port of London there is established a General Registrar and Record Office of Seamen, under charge of the Registrar General, who is appointed by the Board of Trade. In order to assist him in the registry of all persons who serve in ships, every master of a vessel the crew of which is discharged in the United Kingdom must make out and sign a list containing the following particulars :—First, the number and date of the ship's register and her registered tonnage ; secondly, the length and general nature of the voyage or employment ; thirdly, the Christian names, surnames, ages, and places of birth of all the crew, their qualities on board, their last employment, and the date and place of shipment ; fourthly, the names of any members of the crew who have died or who have otherwise ceased to belong to the ship, with the wages due them, together with all the attendant circumstances of death, desertion, etc. ; fifthly, the names of any of the crew who have been maimed ; sixthly, the name, age and sex of every person not of the crew who has died on board ; seventhly, similar data of births ; and eighthly, every marriage on board.

These lists are forwarded through the superintendent
before whom the crew is discharged, and in the case
of foreign-going ships must be handed in within
forty-eight hours after the ship's arrival at her final
port or upon the discharge of the crew, whichever
first happens, under a penalty of £6 for every default. Besides this all officers of the customs are ordered to detain any such ship unless the master
produces a certificate from the superintendent that
his list has been forwarded. A similar list must be
delivered, under like penalties, by the master of any
home trade ship within twenty-one days after June
30th and December 31st in every year, thus enabling
a complete record of every British seaman to be
kept, and giving the government power not only to
exercise a judicious control over a most important
class of its producers, but to form some just opinion
of its resources for any emergency which may arise
either in peace or war.

Under the act ships include every description of
vessel used in navigation not propelled by oars ;
they are divided into two classes—first, foreign-going ships, which embrace all vessels trading beyond
the limits of the United Kingdom and places situated off its own coast and the islands of Guernsey,
Jersey, Sark, Alderney, and Man, and all that part
of the Continent of Europe between Havre and the
River Elbe ; secondly, home trade ships, which distinguish all vessels the voyages of which are confined to the limits specified above. Foreign-going
ships cannot legally proceed to sea unless the masters, or the first and second or only mates have certificates either of competency or service ; nor home

trade ships unless the masters and first or only mate possess such certificates ; and no ship of any class of 100 tons burden or upward can start on a voyage unless at least one person besides the master has a valid certificate appropriate to his grade. To check fraud every person who ships in any of these grades without such a certificate, or any person who knowingly employs him, or without ascertaining that he has such a certificate, incurs a penalty not exceeding £50 for each offence. The certificate of competency is the one now most in use, especially in the junior grades, and is given to such applicants as pass a set examination and comply otherwise with certain conditions of sobriety, morality, etc. The testimonials of service entitle officers who served either as masters or mates in foreign going ships before January 1, 1851, or on home trade ships before the same date in 1854, to serve in like capacities ; and is further extended to include all officers who obtained the grade of past mate and above in the English naval or the East India Company's service. Any such officer, upon the production of testimonials as to character, is entitled to obtain a certificate as master of a merchant ship. There are similar certificates given to engineers, that of service being for persons who served as first or second class engineers in government or private employ before April, 1862, certain conditions as to the size of the ship and the officers' grades in the latter service determining whether their certificates shall be first or second class. Certificates of competency for a foreign-going ship entitle the holder to the command of any ship, but those for the home trade are rigo-

· 6

rously confined to service in that class. In order to
determine the fitness of applicants rules for the conduct of examinations have been published, and examiners have been appointed by the local boards for
each district. These examiners are rarely over two
in number, and may be selected from either the naval
or merchant service ; though in some cases the one
employed to test the navigation knowledge of an applicant has been a civilian with a special knowledge
of that science and without any sea training. The
examination days are arranged for general conven-
ience, so that a candidate who wishes to go to sea
and misses the day at his own port, may proceed to
another where the Board is in session. Except in
London and Liverpool, where certain hours and
days of the week are made obligatory, candidates
must give their names to the local board on or before the day of examination, and at all times testimonials as to character must be submitted in ample
season to permit their verification at the office of
the Registrar General. In the case of foreigners or
of British seamen serving in foreign vessels, these
testimonials must be officially confirmed by some
authority of the foreign country to which the person or ship belongs, or failing that, by the evidence
of some credible witness.

The grades for which examinations must be
passed are second, only and first mate, master and
extra master in foreign-going ships ; mate and master in home trade ships, and first and second class
engineers in all steamers, with a voluntary examination for all masters and mates in steam. A second mate must be seventeen years of age and have

been four years at sea ; an only mate must be nineteen years of age and have been five years at sea,
and a first mate have the same age and sea service,
with at least one year's experience as second or only
mate. The qualifications demanded of the two
lower grades are those which are supplied by what
is known in this country as a common school education, with some rough knowledge of simple navigation and an acquaintance with signalling. Practical seamanship and the ability to keep an ordinary
watch are also requisite, with an intelligent understanding of life-saving appliances. Added to these a
mate must be able in navigation to observe azimuths
and compute the variation of the compass ; to compare chronometers and to keep their rates, and from
them to find the longitude by observations of the sun,
and to determine the latitude by single altitudes of the
sun off the meridian; finally he must be able to adjust
and use the sextant in all observations. In seamanship
he must give evidence of a superior knowledge, such
as would entitle him to be trusted with the ship in
bad weather, to handle sails, to shift spars, to get in
heavy weights and to stow a hold. A master must
be twenty-one years of age and have been six years
at sea, for two of which at least he must have been
a first and second mate ; his testimonials must be of
a first class character, and added to the qualifications
demanded of a mate, he must be able to find the
latitude by sun and star, to compute the variation of
the compass in all the usual ways, to explain the
law of tides and, from the full and change of the
moon, find the state of the tide at any hour in any
part of the world ; and finally, he must explain the

nature and mode of determining the extent of the attraction of the ship's iron upon the compass. In seamanship he must show a capability to deal with any maritime emergency and to care for his ship under unexpected and perilous circumstances ; he must know how to make jury-rudders, build rafts, and understand signalling so as to tell at a glance their characters and in many cases their meaning without referring to the book ; he must be able to manage mortars and rocket-lines in case of stranding, and be acquainted with the leading lights of the channels he has been accustomed to navigate or which he is likely to employ. He is questioned as to his knowledge of invoices, charter parties and Lloyds' Agents, and besides knowing the nature of bottomry he must possess a sufficient acquaintance with the provisions of law relating to entry, and discharge and management of his crew, and with the penalties and entries to be made in the official log-book. He must, as a matter of conscience, understand his medicine chest, for his *clientéle* lies without the purview of "crowners' quests," and he must be able to mitigate or prevent scurvy on shipboard. An extra master's examination is voluntary and is intended only for persons who desire to obtain certificates of the highest grade. Its demands are quite rigorous and fall below only those practical tests to which ensigns in the navy are subjected.

Looked at broadly all these examinations serve, so far as any examination can, to prove an officer's fitness for the grade to which he aspires. It is claimed that they are loosely conducted and that many incapable candidates pass owing to the carelessness,

venality, or over-indulgence of the examiners; but
from the characters of the men selected for this last
duty it may be safely argued that the number of applicants who slip through is small.

The Norwegian government has endeavored to
assimilate the condition of the naval and mercantile
services, and has made intellectual attainments obligatory upon the merchant masters. The results
have been to form a sober and an intelligent class,
that has secured the admiration and respect of the
maritime peoples. It is not unfrequent that naval
lieutenants obtain permission to command merchantmen, and public policy there, as it should everywhere, dictates that masters and mates should be men
of education and special training, qualified for useful and brilliant service to their country in time of
need. Under this centralized system most excellent
results have been attained. And it is only where such
exist that maritime success may be assured.

What then are we to expect when we have no
tests, and it rests only with the ship-owner to determine who shall be intrusted with property of which
his share may be the smallest part? In England
they are striving every day to advance the scheme
of examinations, and to eradicate faults which they
claim arise more from the lowness of the standard
than from any other pregnant cause. It certainly
would add to the efficiency of the merchant marine
and increase the prestige of its officers if a broader
examination were required. Not only should it be
made to include the highest seamanship and all
practical navigation, but, according to Brassey, at
least one foreign language and the elements of a

commercial education. If a moderate annual stip-
end were given to those who passed an examination
in gunnery, the officers would be encouraged to prepare themselves in peace for the duties war might
require. With us especially would all these tests be
necessary. Our navy, at the best, is a skeleton, upon
which with material drawn from the merchant marine we must build a vivified personality that would
aid us in asserting every right external violence or
greed might assail. The higher examinations would
tend to secure more uniform excellence, for even
now, under existing rules, the captains of the largest
ships are unequal in character and skill. It is not
necessary that this proposed extension of the scope
of requirements should be in the line of abstruse
mathematics ; but naval architecture, modern lan-
guages and commercial knowledge, whether relating
to law, foreign exchange, or general trade, would
scarcely be less useful than the mathematical theory
of navigation.

Here then in England is a system founded upon
principles of equity, justice, and usefulness, suited to
our necessities and not antagonistic to our national genius and instinct ; a plan so practical
that no individual effort is hampered, and yet so
theoretical that the mere man of straw, whose fitness rests only upon what his experience of facts
may reach, and not upon what his grasp of principles may assert, is sure to find a level where his
possibilities for harm are reduced to a minimum.
We can adopt it with safety, for it grew out of those
same necessities of the modern spirit which affect
our civilization ; it is based upon intelligence and

education ; its success justifies its existence, and its progress gives surety of its permanence.   Fortified by the knowledge of the good it has effected in England we can urge its adoption here, and as we must begin at a beginning that is not as yet, and fight our way up to the point already attained by nations lacking those maritime activities so essential to commercial supremacy that we possess, it is our duty and should be our pride to anticipate in the present the demands of a future which can be made glorious for the merchant service.

CHAPTER VIII.

THE TRAINING OF BRITISH SEAMEN.

BUT even with a logical and consistent system of administration, and with effective ships, there can be no permanent nor profitable maritime success unless there are good sailors and officers, and a sufficient reserve from which losses may be wholly or in part supplied. Good crews can be obtained only by giving more attention to the physical, mental, and moral condition of sailors. As a creature of romance the hardy tar is a noble being ; as the actual victim of persecution and neglect, he is a deplorable evidence of man's inhumanity. To be even a fairly good sailor requires double the ability demanded by any other of the common pursuits of life, for as Raleigh said, years ago, it is the one which exacts all manner of carnal cunning. It seems reasonable to believe that when the mysteries of the business were once solved, it would be pursued with zest and profit ; and yet in every year over one-third of the losses of skilled mariners is due to the voluntary surrender of a trade which pays better than any other followed by the laboring classes, which is always certain of affording employment, but which has been gained and is maintained only through such infinite misery and sacrifice, that it becomes unbearable. And there is no reason in this, for while it could be brought to

the same plane of comfort and respectability as any
other, it suffers from a neglect almost universal. This
is due partly to misapprehension, partly to carelessness ; for, fairly stated, the attitude of the public
mind toward it is the result more of the observation
of Jack ashore, and of the ignorance of Jack afloat,
than of any belief that the trade is of its nature a
brutalizing one.   In a dim way there is an appreciation of its heroism and of its importance in the modern
scheme, and vaguely it is understood that no life
calls for more manly traits or for greater self-denial.
But, except upon rare occasions, land and sea exis-
tences are nowhere tangent ; and being thus removed from the sphere of active sympathies of those
in whom lie possibilities for his amelioration, what
may be expected of the man before the mast ?

Usually a wanderer from childhood, his home ties
are severed and his home influences weakened ; his
life is spent either on shipboard, in a dull round of
mechanical duties accentuated by moments of terrible peril, or on shore, awaiting a chance to ship
again ; the labors of the one period are swallowed
by the idleness of the other, just as his system pul-
sates between the severe asceticism of the sea and
the nameless debaucheries of the shore ; nowhere
is there a point of rest for the swing of his life-
pendulum, and he has before him the pauper work-
house or the sea that is always waiting.

Ashore he lives in a sailor's boarding-house, where
he is robbed and inveigled into all kinds of debauch-
ery while his money lasts or his prospects of getting
a ship will justify the boarding-master in holding
him upon the credit of the advance money.   The

butcher, the baker, and the candlestick-maker may
be idle awaiting business or enjoying relaxation just
so long as their money permits, but that being exhausted, they must work or starve. Not so with the
sailor ; for his credit is so good and his absolute value,
based upon supply and demand, is so great that he
may be kept as sheep are kept, penned in a market
of horrors, awaiting the highest bidder, who always
comes. Finally he is shipped, and joins his vessel
usually half starved, half clothed, entirely impecun-
ious and wholly drunk. And when he is recalled to
a practical appreciation of the beauties of life by a
backhander from the mate who is stowing the anchors, he finds himself outside Sandy Hook, bound
for a deep-water voyage and with two months' earnings, yet to be gained, all gone in advance. Here is
what several experienced ship masters testified to
before the Congressional Committee, though these
are matters of such every-day occurrence as to excite
no more interest, even in shipping circles, than the
sudden foundering of an ocean-tramp would arouse
among the dervishes howling outside the mosques
of Cairo.

Captain B. S. Osgood, who had twenty-five years'
experience at sea, said "it was a fact that ninety
per cent. of the engaged sailors went on board
drunk. What was needed was a law to blot out the
legalized boarding-house master. The so-called
philanthropy that went about the country collecting money, and that turned out nothing but books
and tracts, was not the kind of philanthropy required for the sailor. No sailor, no matter how good
he might be and how much money he had, could

come there (into the Fifth Avenue Hotel). He and his baggage would not be received. He had to go to the boarding-house, where he was robbed, and New York State legalized it. His son that day was in an English ship, because he could not with decency sail in an American vessel. 'Blood money' was the cause of it. 'Blood money' meant paying for an opportunity to go into a ship. It was divided between the boarding-house keeper, the master of the ship, and in many instances with the owner of the vessel. The charge was $5 per capita in this port. There was a time (but many years ago) when he, with others, marched down to the port and they were selected by the captain of the ship for their certificates of good character and for their physique. Now they had to go through a system of red tape. They went, say, to the top of Cherry Street, and were picked out as it suited the boarding-house keeper, and not as it suited the captain ; and even when the sailor was supposed to be guarded by all the safeguards of the law he was robbed. Witness' son had had his name erased from a list because he would not pay the blood money, while dozens of men were shipped before him. That, he thought, was a case for the District Attorney."

"In most cases," continued another witness, "ship-owners received much of the blood money that had been so much talked of. That fact he was positive of." He gave an interesting description of the sailors themselves, instigated by landlords, appearing in crowds in his office, wearing some distinctive mark by which the captain of the vessel would know they were of the blood-money paying circle.

The captain picked these men out in preference to others who were not in the ring, and the Commissioner's efforts to "shut down" on the blood-money system were by this ingenious method frustrated. Still another gave several examples of what sailors call "shanghaing"—that is, kidnapping—stating that men of all professions were forced on board as sailors, so that the boarding-house master might get the "advanced wages." He had known a Catholic priest to have been "shanghaied." The notes by which the money was obtained were forged. As far back as May, 1857, the Chamber of Commerce took up the question of advance wages and decided to move for its abolition, but in one week they were compelled to "back down by the landlords, who had the sailors completely under their control."

This is the sailor's life on shore, and it is better on shipboard only because it is sober and of some value in a world which expects work from everybody; though this last consideration loses much of its unquestionably logical force, when weighed from a head-boom by the seaman who is stowing the jib on a dark night, in freezing weather, off the Cape. As a rule the sailor lives in a murky den which figures in innumerable sea ditties as "the folk'sle, blessed scene of jollity"; and he eats rations which are beautiful to look at when stated in nicely ruled schedules and provided for in mandatory scales, and yet are nothing less than abominations when actually served out from the greasy galley. Attaining with such a life the grand results which the commerce of the world, and our expanding civilizations prove, what could not be hoped for under a more favorable environ-

ment? What would he be, even if the least of the
things vouchsafed by the old Hippocratic formula
to the worst of men,—pure air, good water, and
sunshine—were not denied him to some degree?
Nothing could be worse for a blue-jacket, or for his
less ornamental but equally useful brother of the
merchant service, than coddling; but there is some-
where that golden mean which would make out of
shambling, dissatisfied, but splendid animals, respected and self-respecting members of society. Improve ships and crew accommodations especially; insist upon educated and humane officers; punish a
sea-bully as you would a wife-beater, with hard
labor and innumerable dozens of the cat—for he is
the greatest coward on the earth and sea; teach Jack
in the forecastle that there is something higher and
holier for him than passing weather-earrings and
riding down foretacks all his days; in one word, give
him the half-chance which has usually been denied
him from the day of his birth, and then judge what
his possibilities may be. It can be done, it is being
done now in some degree. What a common humanity has failed to enforce, the jingling shillings, the
nimble sixpences have brought about; and of all
nations England, as that one most nearly affected, is
foremost in the new departure.

These simpler things are ordered differently there,
though of course the absolute state of affairs is good
only by contrast with the evil of the management
here. A few of the provisions of the General Act
and its amendments are as follows: No fees are exacted for the engagement and discharge of seamen;
no seaman has the power to assign or dispose of

his wages, but must receive them himself ; no debt
exceeding five shillings, incurred by any seaman
after engaging to serve, is recoverable until the service is concluded ; good boarding-houses under wise
control are offered him to choose from ; lodging-
house keepers charging a seaman for a longer time
than he owes, are liable to a penalty of $50.00 for
each offence ; and in brief, by the enactment of an
admirable law, the rights of sailors are jealously
guarded, and so far as human wisdom can effect,
every precaution is taken for their welfare afloat
and ashore ; for their present life, and for those evil
days to come when they are sure to become a burden either upon their past savings, or lacking them,
upon the charities which are so sparingly doled out
to men of the sea. Like this country, England discovered that her supply of native seamen was dimin-
ishing ; unlike us, she is trying to remedy the disease, for it is a malady of most malignant type. In
1851 the number of foreigners in British ships was
5,793 out of a total of 141,937, or about 4.2 per cent. ;
in 1876 this had grown to 20,911 out of a total of
198,638, or 11.76 per cent.; and to-day nearly 13 per
cent. of the crews in British vessels consist of aliens.
In 1876, of the total mentioned above 125,811 were
employed in sailing vessels and 78,827 in steamers ;
10 per cent. of the former and 50 per cent. of the
latter belonging to the class of stewards, firemen,
etc., seafaring persons who are not sailors, thus
leaving of the seamen class about 150,000 for the
supply of the various vessels. In the grand total
for the year there was a loss of about 16,000 persons,
not quite one-third of these being due to deaths and

the remainder to desertions and to relinquishments
of the trade.   The vessels afloat under the British
flag require over 20,000 officers, 3,000 of these being
for vessels of above 800 tons register, that is for a
class of ships needing men of more than average
skill and intelligence.   The annual loss is nearly
1,000, 50 per cent. of which is credited to deaths—a
striking exemplification of the rigorous nature of
the business.   Out of a whole number of deaths for
the year (officers and men) of 4,151, 2,270 were
caused by drowning, 1,237 of these being in ship-
wrecks.

To replace these losses of crews and officers
several sources of supply are open ; for the re-
newal of losses among the men there are apprentices, volunteers, and boys from the training ships.
To meet the demands for the officers there are four
classes eligible : seamen or machinists competent
for promotion ; cadets qualified by training afloat
in sea-going ships or from the two merchant-train-
ing ships ; volunteers from English or alien navies,
and volunteers from other merchant services.

In the case of the men, apprentices are divided
into two classes : those taken by the owner or master free or upon payment of a bounty, and those
supplied by the Guardians or Overseers of the Poor,
any of whom, in every Union, "may put out and
bind as an apprentice any boy who, or whose parent
or parents is or are receiving relief in such Union,
and who has attained the age of twelve years and
is of sufficient health and strength, and who consents
to be so bound."   These facts must be attested to in
the presence of the boy before two justices of the

peace ; the expenses of his outfit is charged to the Union to which he belongs, and he is assigned a number and a certificate by the Registrar General of Seamen. Volunteers are such persons as the master and owner may consent to receive on board as part of the crew ; the regulations governing their shipment have been mentioned before, and as a rule the class is so. efficient that, in the relative manning of British and American steamers carrying mails, freights and passengers, there is, under the English flag, one man to every 70½ tons, and under ours one to every 40½ tons. In steamers carrying freight only, the British have one man to every 51 tons, and we have one to every 40½, showing that there is not undermanning but a superior quality of seamanship.

It is generally accepted as a sea maxim that the best way to make a sailor is to begin early ; in the British naval service the age at which an applicant may enter is between fifteen and sixteen and a half years, a boy exceeding this last limit being regarded as too mature to adopt readily a life which makes such a radical change on all demands, mental and physical, previously known. This seems wrong, for no boy under seventeen should be taken purely because of the physical harm that is done ; it ought to be added that in this the weight of opinion is against the writer, and he must be contented in sharing his belief with physicians generally and with a few officers abroad who have no control of naval training. To give this education and discipline there are in Great Britain nineteen ships, none under naval administration, and all employed for the supply of sea-·

men to the British Mercantile Marine, and under
certain conditions to the Naval service ; these are
stationed at various suitable points on the coast, generally where the opportunities for most easily drain-
ing a district of its available recruits are best, or where
the overplus of a pauper or homeless class coming
within the intention of particular schools, makes their
presence most necessary. A broad generalization
includes these vessels in three classes, though they
overlap in certain directions : first, reformatory
schools ; secondly, industrial schools ; and thirdly,
schools for the laboring classes. The total pupil
capacity is about 4,500 and the average number always on board under instruction is not far from
4,000. Three ships are purely reformatory schools—
the Akbar and the Clarence, stationed near Liverpool, and the Cornwall, in the Thames. Eleven are
industrial schools—the Cumberland, off Garelock,
Scotland ; the Formidable, off Bristol ; the Gibraltar,
off Belfast ; the Havannah, off Cardiff ; the Mars, on
the Tay ; the Southampton, off Hull ; the Wellesley,
in the Thames, and the Clio and the Mount Edge-
combe. In addition to these there is the Endeavor,
which is defined in Brassey's book to be "a land
training brig, at Feltman." The Arethusa, the Chichester, the Exmouth, and the Warspite are for the
laboring classes generally, and one, the Indefatigable, off Liverpool, is specially intended " for the
sons and orphans of sailors, and for other poor and
destitute boys." Here is a school system which
is unequalled in the world—and here a splendid
charity. The instruction and discipline vary in
the different classes, but briefly recited, it may

7

be said that the tuition is restricted to the elementary branches; that the discipline is rigorous but kindly; and that the food is plain but wholesome; one-half of each day is given to text-books and recitations, the other half to nautical drills and exercises, and there are the usual holidays and vacations.

First in point of age is the Warspite. The society for the administration of this school was founded in 1772 by Jonas Hannaway, and in one hundred and ten years of its existence nearly 60,000 boys were sent by it into the naval and mercantile services. Boys admitted to this ship must be between thirteen and sixteen years of age, and belong to some one of the following classes: 1st. Those who are destitute and without friends. 2d. Those who are in abject distress and are recommended by officers of the society. 3d. Those who have been apprentices charged with petty offences, and who are found unfit for shore apprenticeships; and, 4th. Those who are desirous of going to sea and whose parents are unable to support them. The school is maintained by voluntary offerings, the list of subscribers reaching nearly five hundred, and at times the amount donated exceeds sixty thousand dollars. The boys are not kept for any definite term, but usually the period is two years. In 1880 one hundred and fifty-three boys were sent afloat, principally into the naval service. The Arethusa and Chichester receive the waifs of the London streets, the boys being of extreme youth and cared for as in a Reformatory. The ships are supported by one branch of that great benevolent society of which Lord Shaftesbury is the head, and which has the charge of many hundreds of children of both sexes.

The Formidable, off Bristol, may be taken as an example of the ships under the Industrial Schools Act, to which large grants are made by the general government and special annual allowances are given by the various townships sending boys to the ships.

The regulations for admission to this class are usually as follows :

Boys between the ages of eleven and fourteen will be received on board the Formidable, if sent by magistrates with a medical certificate of fitness for a sailor's life, and approved by the committee under the following sections Of the Industrial Schools Act :

CLAUSE 14.—Any person may bring before two justices or a magistrate any child, apparently under the age of fourteen years, that comes within any of the following descriptions, namely :

That is found begging or receiving alms (whether actually or under the pretext of selling or offering for sale any thing), or being in any street or public place, for the purpose of so begging or receiving alms.

That is found wandering and not having any home or settled place of abode, or proper guardianship, or visible means of subsistence.

That is found destitute, either being an orphan or having a surviving parent who is undergoing penal servitude or imprisonment.

That frequents the company of reputed thieves.

The justices or magistrates before whom a child is brought as coming within one of those descriptions, if satisfied on inquiry of that fact, and that it is expedient to deal with him under this act, may order him to be sent to a certified industrial school.

CLAUSE 15.—Where a child, apparently under the age of twelve years, is charged before two justices or a magistrate with an offence punishable by imprisonment or a less punishment, but has not been in *England* convicted of felony, or in *Scotland* of theft, and the child ought, in the opinion of the justices or magistrate (regard being had to his age and to the circumstances of the case), to be dealt with under this act, the justices or magistrate may order him to be sent to a certified industrial school.

Boys who do not come under one of these clauses, and who therefore cannot be sent by a magistrate's order, will be received into the school, if those who are interested in them are willing to contribute £18 per annum for each boy ; and provided also that the boy is physically fitted for a sailor's life, and is willing to be bound to remain at the school a certain period and go to sea when a ship is selected for him. His age must be between eleven and fourteen, and he must also be approved by the committee and its medical officer.

The Exmouth is a school for boys of the poorest class, who are sent to it by the Boards of the Unions (almshouses) of the metropolitan districts of London ; they are received at any time between the ages of nine and fifteen and a half, and are obliged to leave when they arrive at the age of sixteen or sixteen and a half; the largest number received on board are between twelve and thirteen years of age. They are instructed in the elementary English branches, seamanship, swimming, small-arm, cutlass, great-gun drill, and singing. All boys are taught to cut, make, and mend their own clothing. A band with a complement of fifty-eight is kept up, and certain boys are given instruction in carpentering and in cooking ; the latter, a most excellent idea, receiving especial attention.

Attached to the ship is a small brigantine, which is used for practical training underway. She cruises in the mouth of the Thames between April and Oc-

tober ; the complement of boys on board is thirty,
ten being changed every week, so that they are
always twenty oldsters to ten new hands. The more
important instructions on board this tender are :
keeping careful watch by night when at anchor ;
mooring and unmooring ; loosing and making sail,
and reefing and furling under all conditions ; steer-
ing ; a thorough knowledge of conning terms ; heav-
ing-to and picking up boats ; heaving the log and
lead ; handling anchors ; and practical teaching of
the rule of the road in a crowded river.

From 1876 to 1879, 876 boys were admitted ; 202
sent to sea ; 29 transferred to the army as musicians ;
90 discharged by order of the Boards of the Unions
from which they came ; 3 given other situations ; 5
absconded, and 2 died. These boys would in most
cases have formed a part of the great pauper class of
England ; but instead, owing to well-directed charity
and through the expenditure of very little money,
they are lifted to a plane the possibilities of which
by comparison are limitless.

The Indefatigable, which is moored in the Mersey,
off Liverpool, has for its object the training of the
orphans and sons of seafaring men connected with
the port of Liverpool, and of boys whose parents
may be unable to support them. Preference is given
always to the former class. The ship depends entirely upon contributions and subscriptions for its support, and a considerable amount of money is paid
into its treasury by American passengers on board
of English steamers between New York and Liverpool, who thus contribute, in most cases without
knowing, to a most praiseworthy charity.

The committee of management comprises some of
the most prominent names of Liverpool, most of the
great ship-owners being represented.   The mayor of
Liverpool is president *ex officio.*

GENERAL RULES.

Boys of all religious denominations are eligible for admission.

No boy is received on board under twelve or over fifteen years of
age, nor is any one retained who does not show an aptitude for a sea-
life.

The period during which a boy may remain on board is intended
to be not less than three years.   This period is not extended except
by special sanction of the committee in individual cases.

Life-governors or others willing to contribute not less than £100
to the funds of the institution, or an annual subscription of £10,
have a right to nominate a boy for each such donation.

The general committee, under whose management the ship is,
must consist of not more than forty members.   An executive committee, of not more than ten members, is elected by the general
committee.   The executive committee is obliged to meet twice in
each month, three members forming a quorum.

In a report on the Training of Seamen of England, from which many of these facts are taken,
Lieutenant-Commander Chadwick, U. S. Navy, says :
"Not to be passed over as training-schools for boys
destined for the sea, are the industrial schools such
as that as Feltham, which has taken the foremost
rank as a school of the kind.   It is a reformatory
establishment for convicted boys, and is conducted on
the half-time system.   It is an admirably managed
institution, and Captain Brooks, a retired officer of
marines, has received high praise for the success of
the place.   What makes the mention of it proper
here is that there is in the grounds a brig, built from
the berth-deck upward, upon which the boys, who

have selected a seafaring life, are exercised.   Fifty-six boys were sent to sea from this place last year, six of whom entered the navy as bandsmen, much attention being also given to music.

"This method of having a means of nautical train-ing attached to institutions of this kind is very well thought of. Many boys thus receive sufficient train-ing to fit them to early become good sailors, and a taste for the sea is fostered in a class for which there is too little employment of a fixed kind."

To meet the demands for officers there are two ships, the Conway, anchored off Liverpool, and the Worcester, anchored off London.   These school-ships are employed mainly to train and educate boys for officers of the Merchant Marine, but pupils intended for the Royal Navy are also admitted and receive a special training. On each ship an efficient nautical and civil staff is maintained, and the course, which requires two years, includes mathe-matics as far as spherical trigonometry, the theory and practice of navigation, magnetism, meteorol-ogy, and such seamanship as can be acquired on board ship at an anchorage; this last, it is true, may not be much, but it is of such sufficient value as to warrant the Board of Trade in reckoning the full period as one year spent actually afloat off soundings. Six appointments as midshipmen in the Royal Naval Reserve are annually granted to the Conway; posi-tions as apprentice leadsmen in the Bengal Pilot service are allotted the graduates; and many ship-owners give such a preference to these cadets over all other apprentices as to take them into their em-ploys without the customary fee of indenture.   No

boy is received under the age of twelve and none
over sixteen ; the terms of admission are fifty guineas
per annum, and for this board, tuition, medical attendance, uniform and outside clothing are supplied.
The boys belong to an exceptionally good class, and
it argues well for the merchant marine that the sons
of many distinguished and influential men should be
acquiring the elements of an honorable profession
under circumstances which, before many years, will
result in the best English vessels being commanded
by officers in no wise inferior to their brother sailors
of the government marine.   The capacity of both
ships is about 300, and this number as a rule is maintained on board.

Under these general methods of supply the losses
of the British merchant marine are made good ; the
training ships, of course, yield the smallest percentage, but they give a nucleus which will absorb gradually the more important duties of the service.   The
annual returns for one year are compiled here, in
order to show the number of boys sent into the merchant service by each class of ships, the average
cost of maintenance, and the sources whence the
revenues for the support of the system are derived.

"The great defect of the mercantile training system now in use in England is that too many of the
vessels are mere reformatories, which send into the
service boys with bad antecedents.   Too great a
supply of such boys tends to cast a stain upon the
profession, and causes it to be looked upon as a
refuge for the destitute, worthless, and vagabond
class.   The great aim ought to be to elevate it as a
reputable calling ; to make men think and feel that

Class of ships.	Number of each.	Number of boys sent into the merchant service.			Average expense of each boy on board, per head, per annum.
		As apprentices.	In other capacities.	Total number.	£ s. d.
For officers	2	105*	7	112	53 15 0
Industrial schools	8	109	291	400	18 19 7½
Independent ships	4	147	479	626	21 6 2
Reformatories	3	Nil†	168	168	20 7 8
Grand total, number of boys sent into the merchant service				1,306	

* These are not seaman apprentices, but officers. † All boys being under detention are sent to sea on license, under the reformatory act.

Expenses of Maintenance.

Class of ships.	No. of each.	Receipts.			Total receipts.	Total expenditure.
		Public vote.	Private subscriptions.	Pupils' fees.		
		£ s. d.	£ s. d.	£ s. d.	£ s. d.	£ s. d.
For officers	2	......	127 0 0	13,492 10 0	13,619 10 0	13,755 0 0
Industrial schools	8	38,246 16 11	4,400 19 1*	......	42,647 16 0	33,017 5 9‡
Independent ships	4	......	10,942 15 3†	......	10,942 15 3	24,184 15 11
Reformatories	3	12,861 0 0	593 0 0	......	13,454 0 0	13,731 0 0

* This is the amount received by 7 ships.   † This is the amount received by 3 ships.   ‡ This is the amount spent by 7 ships.

it is as respectable as any other manual labor ; the general thought of parents being that for a boy to go to sea is to go entirely to the bad. This latter feeling, of course, is strengthened in the service itself, where too many of a depraved class are sent from reformatory institutions and houses of refuge. The aim ought rather to be to attract volunteers to the training ships, and not, as in too many cases in England, require that the boy should be a pauper before he can have the advantages and facilities afforded by these vessels." (Chadwick.)

In some measure this is true ; but it goes too far, for, on the other hand, the new influences are wholesome, and though the best material may not be obtained, yet certain classes are reached, the large majorities of which are saved from crime and pauperism. Many of these boys have become officers, and in the great mass the evil tendencies of those who are distinctly criminal, as opposed to the instincts of others who are merely poor, cannot counteract the permanent good which the force of example and the restraint of discipline produce. It is certain that crime is less prevalent, and that ships are better manned and handled than ever before.

But what are we doing to make good the losses which, by the same operations of the economic law, fall upon our merchant marine. We have one ship, the St. Mary's, stationed at the Port of New York and supported mainly by the city government. The results of her services have been good, but these are necessarily of the most limited character. In eight years there were 896 entries and 328 graduates ; of these, 228 went to sea ; 70 non-graduates also adopted a seafaring life, and of the whole number perhaps 60 have become officers. Are we prepared to let this matter rest here ? Our legislative bodies, and, failing them, our merchants, and as a last resource, our charitable people, must study these factors and attempt to solve the problems into which they enter. New and accepted theories make rigorous demands upon us, and the schools which gave us the capable seamen of the first half of this century are inadequate to satisfy the requirements of these later days. As a last word, it must be emphasized that even if our shipping were restored, we have neither the men nor the officers to man it ; and this under a civilization which insists upon a skilled merchant marine, governed, equipped, and educated in accordance with modern ideas, as the only hope of successful competition for the commerce of the world.

CHAPTER IX.

THE NAVY AND THE MERCHANT MARINE.

THE relation between the navy and the merchant marine is not always apparent to the non-professional reader, but no law of the economic question is better defined ; commercial supremacy and naval power have gone hand in hand in all countries, and though it is conceded the former should precede, yet we once made the mistake of permitting commerce to develop without commensurate additions to our naval strength, and to our great disadvantage. Had an adequate force been at the disposition of the government in 1861, the ports of the seceding States would have been seized before they could have been placed in a defensive condition ; not a blockade runner could have entered ; not a rover have escaped to prey upon our commerce ; and those fitted out elsewhere would have been cut short in their careers of destruction. Still further, the decadence of our commerce, though not the outgrowth of the civil war, would have been arrested, and long ere this we might have entered upon that policy of revival which we are bound to pursue. Trade is gained and influence maintained in China and Japan by the nations which keep powerful naval forces on those coasts. The Pacific commerce belongs naturally to us, but despite our proximity the flag is rarely seen off the western coast, and our intercontinental trade barely suffices to employ one line of steamers. We are the great middle kingdom, and an analysis of the laws underlying trade expansion proves incontrovertibly that we should rule the commerce of the world. Our enormous productive surplus demands new markets, and to foster and develop a commerce based upon conditions of supply, demand, and direct and easy means of transportation, we must have an efficient and powerful war marine. Every ship should become a commercial agent, and the dissemination of information upon the resources of the country, the prices and values of our commodities, the advantages inuring to foreign merchants by dealing with us—in short, a realization of the work laid down for the Ticonderoga in her last cruise ought to form an essential part of the orders of cruising men-of-war.

The duty of all navies is beyônd everything else to guard the territory of its country ; next to protect its natural commerce ; and then to police and survey the seas in the general interests of humanity. When the naval service is not altogether neglected, it is treated from a standpoint where absolute and special knowledge are wanting, and it is a common complaint that of no other branch of the government service does there exist so little general information. A generally accepted, but none the less erroneous, idea is that its duties are confined almost exclusively to offensive and defensive operations during hostilities ; that in peace it is a luxury, partly justified, perhaps, in the shadowy maxim of accepted statesmanship that peace should prepare for war. With

us there is a blind dependence upon what is called
the creative possibility of the nation.   Little serious
examination is given to the subject, and with experts
only is there a full appreciation of the ignorance of
and the want of anything more than a sentimental interest in the navy of the country.   To cruise between
pleasant ports, to show the flag in the strongholds
of nations that respectfully hint their acquaintance
with our tremendous possibilities of aggression, and
then, the novelty of the cruise being exhausted, to
return to navy yard and dry dock and, about election
time, afford employment to swarms of unskilled
henchmen of ambitious politicians—these, and only
these, make up the popular belief of the duties of a
modern man-of-war in time of peace.   Occasionally
the national conscience is stirred by the recital of
the low plane to which our service has fallen, and of
the advances which are being made abroad ; a pale
glimmer of interest is excited, the conditions are
hazily discussed, and the responsibility and blame
being relegated to Congress, where they belong, all
public interest in the subject ends. At times there are
a few critics who demand the extinction of the service,
its necessity for any reasons being denied ; this is
usually supplemented with the assertion that in war,
a navy sufficient and capable could be created with
the same readiness, and raised to the same standard
of excellence in the same time, as could a volunteer
army.   As a concession to the prejudices of less destructive minds, the reformers are willing to employ
a few skilled officers who will keep alive the embers
of naval knowledge, much as the laborious monks
preserved those of ancient letters during the Middle

Ages.   Foreign squadrons are branded, from the ex-
tra-professional standpoint, as useless because we
have no interests abroad, and this being disproved,
the home squadron is assailed, presumably because
we have no interests at home.   As much of this
hypercriticism arises from ignorance, it is only fair
to show what are the duties demanded of a navy in
time of peace ; wherein these are satisfied by our
squadrons ; the connection between the navy and
the merchant marine ; in what direction naval usefulness may be extended, and what claims the home
squadron has for extension and development as the
most important naval division.

Peace has its naval duties no less than war, and
none the less onerous nor honorable are the demands
it makes upon the skill, intelligence, fearlessness,
and readiness of resource, which are the essential
characteristics of the seaman.   At home the complex
machinery of the law and the force of communal
interest protect the citizens, but upon the high seas
and in foreign countries his life and happiness are
assailable save for the protection vouchsafed by the
navy of his country.   So much was this principle
recognized by the framers of the Constitution that
the navy was given a permanent, in contradistinc-
tion to the temporary character of the army, the
Constitution expressly declaring that Congress shall
have power "to *raise* and *support* armies," and "to
provide and *maintain* a navy."   Armies have sometimes subverted the liberties of a country, navies
never, and in some countries, notably England, the
navy is, for the reason of its superior importance, the
senior service.   War is never absent from the calcu-

lations of the civilized nations, and barbarism, respecting nothing but force, repels alike interference,
association, and instruction. In every sea-port of
Europe ; in Asia, to the head of unnamed rivers on
the confines of the Chinese Empire ; in Japan ; in
the islands and among the groups of the Southern
seas, our citizens claim and need protection. Abroad
they are found occupying every field which enterprise dares invade or energy avails to conquer ; and
everywhere they carry with them those affirmative
and sometimes aggressive ideas of freedom and
progress which are antagonistic to the traditions,
customs, and practices of local governments; our
progressive civilization is apparent in every land our
countrymen penetrate, and we can afford to neglect
neither our responsibilities as a representative nation, nor our obligations to the people who claim our
countenance and the protection of the flag. Thus
our navy vivifies, asserts, and develops the idea of
republicanism as the vital factor in contemporary
civilization.

Navies are the police of the world ; they carry
the strong arm of the law into the remotest regions ;
they empanel themselves as jurors to decide the fact
and sit in judgment upon wrong-doers ; zealously
and with great sacrifice they guard the well-being of
citizens whose happiness and liberty without them
would be wholly insecure; and they project civilization into lands which are benighted, first by the influence of the moral idea, and then, if necessity arise,
by those energies that, after all, most appeal to the
savage or semi-barbaric mind. The spirit of piracy
exists now as ever, and there are no pirates, or piracy

is rare, because the seas are policed by the war vessels of the world.

It is not germane here to consider the necessities which may appeal to a maritime country during conditions of belligerency or alliance; but at all times such a nation is subject to the demands which neutrality may make. These require that no aid prejudicial to the warlike status of other countries shall be given to one of the belligerents beyond, of course, the requirements of a common humanity; that the citizens of the neutral must not supply a belligerent with articles recognized as contraband of war; that warlike operations within its territory must be forbidden, and that in belligerent countries the life and property of its citizens must be guarded and its commerce protected from unjust or burdensome interferences. The determined stand we took upon the Alabama claims pledges us irrevocably to the acceptance of these terms, and yet without the possession of an effective fleet contingencies may arise under any of these conditions which might imperil the national honor.

Under circumstances of perfect amity a nation is bound to preserve the friendly relations which exist and to strive for a peaceful adjustment of all differences; citizens or foreigners within its territory must be kept from violating the laws which forbid active aid being given to foreign insurrection or rebellion; arbitrary acts of reprisal must be prevented; the lives and property of its citizens must be guarded from mobs or the dangers of insurrections within the territory of a friendly nation; foreigners must be warned against the performance of arbitrary acts injurious to

8

commercial rights; assistance must be given to the survey of the highways of commerce ; a correct knowledge of the coasts of the world must be obtained by exploring and surveying expeditions, and no legitimate means must be spared to foster and to extend those'commercial interests which are essential factors of national happiness and prosperity.

Fortunately the theory of our government is one of extreme reserve as to foreign affairs, and it would be the commission only of some overt act which would justify a display of naval strength as a means of awakening the serious attention of an offending nation to a question in dispute ; still the zeal of our consular service, whether arising from misdirected devotion to the old flag and an appropriation, or from the claims of friendship or private business, is apt at times to call for the exercise of the wisest discretion in treating what are popularly called outrages. From the general policy of non-intervention in questions outside our territory must be excepted the Monroe doctrine ; by its moral force the Spanish colonies of Central and South America were aided to gain and have since been able to maintain their independence. The reassertion of its principles at a time when advantage was taken of internal dissension to violate it, and the subsequent display of a trained army and an effective fleet forced France to leave Mexico. And to-day we can be no more willing to abandon our position than when our resources were most weakened. Foreign Powers must not interfere between combatants on this continent, even under the specious plea of humanity, and we cannot permit any other country to assume control of a canal the ʼ

unfriendly possession of which would be a menace
in time of war and a denial of inherent and vital
commercial rights in days of peace. Covetous eyes
are said to be cast upon outlying islands and seaports of Central America, and at least two of the
Continental Powers are searching for new colonial
stations on our coasts, which would form flanking
positions and rendezvous in war, and commercial
points of attack in peace.

Such, briefly stated, are some of the duties which
our relations to other nations impose upon us ; but
besides these there are others no less imperative,
and the fulfilment of which gives greater power for
home and foreign defence. Twenty-five years since
the approaches to our Atlantic coast were the most
dangerous in the world ; but to-day, so far as the
hydrographic work of naval officers can be operative,
they are as safe as any others of equal importance ;
but these charts and sailing directions require constant care and verification owing to the shifting of
channels through the effect of winds and currents,
and hence this work must be permanent from its
vital relation to commerce. Our lighthouse establishment is the largest in the world, and the successful administration of this immense interest is being
conducted mainly by naval officers, with an efficiency
and economy which make it the admiration of other
governments. The education of officers and men is
zealously cared for—that of the former at the Naval
Academy, an institution the methods of which are so
admirable as to have gained for it the highest award
of the Paris Exhibition. The instruction of the men
is an element of the greatest value, for it has been

found impossible to supply in time of peace the navy
with seamen drawn from other services or from the
merchant marine ; and our government, like others,
has been forced to establish training ships, where
youths are drilled in the duties and subjected to the
discipline which will make them, with their officers,
coequally useful servants of the Republic. Navy
yards and other shore stations, boards of inspection
and examination, the manufacture and supply of ordnance and of equipment stores, the Naval Observa-
tory, the Bureaus of the Navy Department, the Torpedo Station and other important and special duties
claim the services of naval officers. And notwithstanding that the list of officers is 336 less than it
was forty years since, and that the country has grown
from seventeen to fifty millions, inhabiting a territory
increased by the whole Pacific coast, it may be safely
asserted that, under like claims upon its resources,
no other department of the government can show
a record equally as good.

To carry out effectively all the duties of police,
commercial development, protection, neutrality, exploration, and education of its personnel, the government has assigned its naval force to five divisions :—
First—The North Atlantic. The limits of this station extend from the east coast of North America
to the forty-fifth degree of longitude west, or to
about the meridian of the Grand Banks, and from
any indefinite north latitude to the equator, and
thence in a diagonal line westward along the north-
eastern coast of South America. Within this area,
though not under its direction, are the navy yards
of Portsmouth, Boston, New York, League Island,

Norfolk, and Pensacola, with the naval stations of New London and Beaufort. At present there are five vessels attached to this squadron. Secondly— The European station. This embraces the European, Mediterranean, and African coasts, as far south as St. Paul de Loando ; thence diagonally westward to the junction of the equator and the forty-fifth degree of west longitude, this meridian separating it from the North Atlantic station. Three vessels are attached to the fleet, and there is a storehouse at Villefranche, France. Thirdly—The South Atlantic station. This commences at the southern limit of the European, embraces all the Atlantic coasts of Africa and South America, and extends by a late order beyond the Cape of Good Hope to the 70th degree of east longitude, and as far north as the equator in that quarter. Two ships are attached to the station, and there is a naval depot at Rio Janeiro. Fourthly— The Pacific station. This includes the Pacific coasts of North and South America. North of the equator it extends to the 170th degree of west longitude; south of the line it stretches to the 130th degree of east longitude, then curves northerly so as to embrace the islands east of Borneo, and thence it follows the 115th degree of east longitude to the Antarctic continent. The whole area embraces Australia, Australasia, Polynesia, and part of the Aleutian chain. Six vessels belong to the station, and there is in the north a navy yard at Mare Island, and in the south a storeship at Callao. Fifthly—The Asiatic station. This embraces the east coast of Africa, excluding the waters of the South Atlantic station, the Indian Ocean, and China seas, and the northeast coast of

Asia as far as the 170th degree of west longitude. Six vessels are attached to the station, and there is a storehouse at Nagasaki, in Japan.

Roughly speaking, the Pacific station includes nearly one-half of the whole cruising area, China about one-third, and the others the remaining one-sixth, the proportions being, relatively, Pacific, 7-15; China, 4-15; South America, 2-15, and Europe and the North Atlantic about 1-15 each. Assuming the water space of the world usually given, and rejecting those parts not of necessity subjected to the visits of war vessels, there are over one hundred millions of water square miles to be policed by all the navies, and as our share we contribute twenty-three indifferent vessels. This is absurdly small, and improvement is necessary in the direction of increase, not only of vessels but of squadrons. But in doing this we must remember that extension can be based only upon the needs of commerce-development, and upon the necessity of protection being assured our citizens abroad and at home, the latter being the primary consideration. Our trade with Europe is fixed as to volume, direction, and growth, and all attempts at change must be made in the means, the vehicles of transportation. Commerce with Japan, China, and Brazil can be profitably secured, though its development will be of slower growth, owing in the East to the Oriental theory of governments that the land should support the people, and, because in all these countries of the limits inevitably imposed by the social, industrial, and economical condition of the importers. Everywhere there is evident less or greater trade development, based upon the true laws of supply and demand, and capable of being fostered by judicious efforts, which under no circumstances mean subsidies or anything out of a fair chance for all our people to compete fairly in the markets of the world. Of course there are substantial obstacles due to our high duties, but the prosperous British colonies will buy our labor-saving machines and commodities if they have a chance, and the absence of discriminative duties leaves the field as open to American as to British merchants.

Beginning, then, with the Pacific fleet, where the area is greatest and commerce development the active principle, it seems necessary to create either two stations, or one station with two divisions, as in 1867-71 ; one assuming the control over all the waters of the old station north of, and the other of all those south of, the equator. To each should be assigned five vessels, the greater area of the southern division and the necessities of Australian trade being compensated for by the extremely and increasingly delicate nature of our relations with the semi-independent British American Dominion of the Northwest, and with the unsettled local governments of Mexico. The Asiatic station should be separated into nearly equal portions, under similar conditions of administration as proposed above, . the southern to be known as the Indian Ocean squadron, and to have assigned to it as cruising grounds the ocean of that name, the Red Sea, the Arabian Gulf, and the Bay of Bengal ; its eastern limits should include Borneo, Sumatra, Java, and all the coast of Australia west of the 120th degree of east longitude. Four vessels should be attached to this squadron with a supply depot upon the mainland. All to the northward of this area should be assigned to the China squadron, and as our citizens have great and necessary interests there, not less than eight vessels should be selected as the effective cruising force.

A glance at the waters of the Atlantic Ocean will show the difficulties that enter into the mutual relations of the European and South Atlantic stations. Apart from the special duties of each, they divide between them the west coast of Africa, the former extending to Loando, the other thence to the Cape. So far as European trade goes the navy can do little toward furthering a development which has already acquired such an unequalled energy. There is no very great danger to the lives or property of our citizens in those civilized lands, and it is probable that three ships, upon the plan of a French naval division, would be ample for every demand which use and tradition could make. But outside these limits, from Mogador to the Cape, there are promises of a great and increasing trade. Under the present system, to reach the ports south of Loando, a ship once a year crosses the profitless expanse of the Atlantic from South America, sails down the coast, and then returns to Brazil, the best part of her labor and time being absorbed in reaching a port and seeking a storehouse. It would seem to be in the direction of a wise policy to relegate the patrol of the whole western coast of Africa to the care of the European squadron; for then, beginning at the upper end, the vessels would communicate with the land, like the reciprocal action of a cogwheel, touching at every needful point going and coming, and thus quadrupling, as compared with the present desultory visiting, the opportunities for displaying the flag, settling disputes, and extending commerce. To effect this change the waters of the European station should extend as far west as the 30th degree of west longitude north and south of the equator, and should have assigned to it six vessels, two or more of these being always in the neighborhood of the Cape, and all of them taking regular turns in cruises on both coasts. By this change the area of the South Atlantic station would be narrowed, and three vessels would be sufficient for its needs—at least until a busier future demanded an increase.

The North Atlantic station is that upon which our main defence rests, and should have not less than nine vessels. In home waters, besides the commercial opportunities of Mexico, Central and South America, and of the contiguous islands, our relations are such that protection to the coast is the paramount duty. The internal conditions of the neighboring countries and the irresistible logic of the history of the past thirty years prove the necessity of constant care and watchfulness. Wars may be foreseen and their exigencies provided for at comparative leisure, but insurrections can never be foretold, and hence the necessity in peace times of an effective squadron, ready to act upon any threatened point at the shortest notice and with the greatest advantage. In the North the disputed questions of the fisheries, the operations of reciprocity treaties, and the dormant idea of annexation should never be absent from our

calculations, for the history of British American relations shows a singular alternation of equitable and
aggressive dispositions toward the interests of the
United States, and notably at seasons when they have
been most hampered by other complications. France
and Austria, assisted at first by Spain and England,
have in the past made a serious assault upon our
only asserted policy ; and to-day some of the trading
nations are seeking not only new markets but new
colonies in the vicinity of our coasts. In the West
Indies we have our hereditary interests in Cuba and
the remembrance of difficulties not only unatoned
for, but which are believed abroad, notably in the
Virginius case, to have been settled by an abject
apology on our part to Spain. All about us are
islands the diverse ownerships of which are liable,
from European complications, to place us in a position of neutrality. We cannot give up our influence with nor our interest in the South and Central
American republics, struggling as they are, slowly
but surely, to the vantage grounds of constitutional
liberty and progress. Nor can we view with indifference the control either of the Panama Canal or
Transisthmian Railway, both of which will be as
much a part of the commercial future of this country
as any of the Pacific Railroads. The necessity of
acquiring coaling stations and rendezvous for our
fleets in tropical waters is another element requiring
careful attention, and we must awaken to the reality
that traditions against outlying possessions are at
this stage of our history simply imbecile, and are
worthy only a country poor in resources and
trembling in abject fear of some great naval power.

Here, then, at home lie the very greatest of our
needs and dangers, and here most liable to appear
are the circumstances which demand a fleet.   The
defence of our coasts is our first duty, and opportunities should be afforded officers to acquire the knowledge essential to that end.   Stretching a distance of
3,000 miles, its demands are enormous, for the stra-
tegic possibilities of the different basins as points of
attack, defence, and support ought to be tested and
the acquaintance with these home waters by the
average sea officer should be that of the intelligent
coast pilot, supplemented by the special acquisitions
which his combatant duties require.   In turn each
of the five great Gulfs from Maine to the Rio Grande
should be studied by a squadron of exercise, and all
the dispositions for its defence, and all its capabilities
as a point of attack and support, should be made plain
under circumstances as nearly analogous to those of
actual war as possible ; in brief, here, upon our own
coast, should be assembled a fleet worthy of the
name, and to it every vessel fitted out at any Eastern
port should be sent for the first six months of a
cruise, and be subjected to its discipline and instruction.   Twice a year, in some one of the great bays,
all the vessels should be assembled for those drills
and exercises which infuse a healthy spirit of rivalry,
give uniformity to routine and organization, and, best
of all, enable our officers to understand intelligently
the inevitable conditions under which modern sea
battles will be fought.

In his report for this year Secretary Chandler declares " There is one measure of national defence
in regard to which the argument cannot be made,

as in the case of ships and guns, that modern discovery is likely to make such improvements in the art of construction that action might for the present be deferred. This is the creation of an interior coast line of water-ways across the head of the peninsula of Florida, along the coast from Florida to Hampton Roads, between the Chesapeake Bay and the Delaware, and through Cape Cod. To these should be added a railroad from the mainland of Florida to Key West. To secure the combined commercial and military advantages which these avenues for merchant and naval vessels would afford, work should be immediately begun and deliberately and economically prosecuted, and not left to be done hastily and expensively in an emergency.

"The United States should not be dependent," he continues, "upon the ports of the great naval powers for coal for the various squadrons in foreign waters. We have already established coaling stations at Honolulu, the Samoan Islands, and at Pichilingue, in Lower California ; and the Monongahela is being fitted for a store-ship at Callao, to hold 1,000 tons of coal. Authority should be asked from Congress to fix the above stations on a firm basis, and to establish additional coaling and naval stations at some or all of the following points : Samana Bay, or some port in Hayti ; Curaçao, in the Caribbean Sea ; Santa Catharina, in Brazil ; the Straits of Magellan ; La Union, in Salvador, or Amapala, in Honduras ; Tullear Bay, in Madagascar ; Monrovia, in Liberia ; the Island of Fernando Po ; and Port Hamilton, in the Nan-how Islands of Corea ; from which latter naval station and the ports of Corea there should

be established a regular line of steamers carrying
the United States flag, connecting with the present
American line between San Francisco and Japan.
Similar stations should in addition be maintained, one
at the best point on the Atlantic side of the Isthmus
of Panama, and another at the Islands of Flamenco,
Perico, Culebra, and Hefiao on the Pacific side, now
owned by American corporations."

To give our navy an effective status, an immediate
increase in the number of our ships is necessary.

In the report of the first Naval Advisory Board it
was asserted that, "taking into proper consideration
the various requirements of the different squadrons
for surveying, deep-sea sounding, protection and
advancement of American commerce, exploration,
protection of American life and property endangered by wars between foreign countries, and service in support of American policy in matters
where foreign governments are concerned, forty-
three unarmored cruising vessels are required constantly in commission, or twelve more than are possibly available now, in case of the most urgent
necessity, both in commission and in reserve. Increasing this number by fifty per centum in order to
obtain a reserve of sufficient strength to maintain
the effectiveness of the fleet, a total of sixty-five vessels is obtained, which would be sufficient were it
not for the fact that the present condition and limited lifetime of some of the vessels included will soon
weaken the number very materially. To allow for
this loss it is the opinion of the Board that five more
vessels should be added, giving a total number necessary to perform efficiently the work of the navy at

present of seventy vessels. Taking from this the thirty-two vessels now available, the Board is of the opinion that thirty-eight unarmored cruising vessels should now be built."

Finally, in August, 1882, and March, 1883, Congress authorized an increase of the navy, and in Mr. Chandler's report to the President, under date of December 1, 1883, he says:

"The three new steel war vessels and the armed despatch steamer authorized at the last session of Congress, which have been named the Chicago, Boston, Atlanta, and Dolphin, are in the course of construction and will be completed, the cruisers within eighteen and the despatch boat within twelve months from the last week in July, 1883. The general dimensions and characteristics of the ships will be as follows :—

	Length.	Breadth.	Draft.	Displacement.	Indicated horse-power.	Estimated sea-speed.	Estimated smooth-water speed.	Capacity of coal-bunkers.	Armament of heavy guns.
	Feet.	Feet.	Feet.	Tons.		Knots.	Knots.	Tons.	
Chicago........	315	48	19	4,500	5,000	14	16	940	14
Boston	270	42	17	3,000	3,500	13	14	580	8
Atlanta........	270	42	17	3,000	3,500	13	14	580	8
Dolphin	240	32	14	1,500	2,300	15	......	310	1

"These vessels represent three main types of unarmored war ships now universally considered as indispensable components of any fleet suitable for general national service upon the high seas. The Chicago is an example of the largest and best unarmored cruising and fighting vessels now built, and will have no superior in the world in the combination of speed, endurance, and armament. In the Boston and Atlanta, speed and endurance have been given full development, while their fighting power has been notably increased by placing the battery in a central superstructure on the spar-deck, and by adopting a brig rig, thereby leaving the extremities clear and unobstructed for fore and aft fire.

"In the Dolphin an important auxiliary in naval operations will be obtained, and she is expected to furnish an excellent model from which may be expanded a high-speed commerce-destroyer, instead of taking as a standard either the overgrown merchant line steamers or the large and expensive despatch vessels which have been built abroad, of questionable utility in time of peace.

"The ships are now under construction in accordance with the Appropriation Acts of August 5, 1882, and March 3, 1883, authorizing such increase of the navy, under the advice and supervision of the Naval Advisory Board. By public advertisement and notice of August 5, 1882, as required by the Act of that date, all designers and builders of ships, marine engines, or ordnance were invited to submit plans of any of the vessels, or any part thereof, within the period of sixty days after August 20th; and further notice was given, November 17th, that such period would be extended up to the time for final decision and action. After the general features of the vessels were indicated by the Board, they were submitted to all shipbuilders likely to make proposals for their construction, with requests for their advice and suggestions concerning the designs, with the view of reaching such final plans and specifica-

tions as would give the best and most effective ships
that could be built.   All plans, models, designs, suggestions, and explanations from any quarter were
fully examined and reported upon by the Board.
The general features and essential requisites of the
ships having been settled by the Department and
the Advisory Board, the plans and specifications were
prepared by the Bureaus of Construction and Repair
and of Steam Engineering; and on May 2, 1883,
advertisements were published, as required by the
Act of March 3, 1883, inviting proposals for their
construction ; these were opened on Monday, July
2d, and all the contracts were on the day following
awarded to the lowest bidder, Mr. John Roach,
of New York City.   The contract for the Chicago
is dated July 26th, with a bond for due completion
in the sum of $500,000 ; the contracts for the
Boston and Atlanta are dated July 23d, with bonds
for $300,000 each ; the contract for the Dolphin is
dated July 23d, with a bond for $150,000.

"The estimates, the contract prices, and the next
lowest bids were as follows :

	Cost estimated by the Advisory Board.	Contract prices.	Next lowest bids.
Chicago.........	$1,248,000	$889,000	$1,080,000
Boston..........	783,500	619,000	650,000
Atlanta	783,500	617,000	650,000
Dolphin.........	399,000	315,000	375,000

showing a total cost for the hull and machinery of
the vessels, including the masts, spars, boats, and
rigging, for preparing which the navy yards are to

be utilized, of $2,440,000, being $774,100 less than the estimates, and $315,000 less than the next lowest bids.

"The statutes authorizing the construction of the cruisers require that they shall be built of 'steel of domestic manufacture, having as near as may be a tensile strength of not less than 60,000 pounds to the square inch, and a ductility in 8 inches of not less than 25 per centum.' Fears were, for a time, entertained that contracts for building the vessels could not be effected at reasonable prices, because of the hesitancy of the steelmakers of this country to bind themselves to furnish the steel required, subject to the scientific and practical tests prescribed by the Advisory Board to insure a compliance with the law. All difficulties have, however, been happily overcome ; and the demonstration that such material can be here produced at moderate cost, is, of itself, of great importance in the progress of our mechanical industries.

" The present condition of our national fleet makes it necessary that the work of reconstruction should be continued as rapidly as a due regard for economy will admit. Accordingly, the Advisory Board submitted a report dated October 25, 1883, of its views as to the new work which should be undertaken in the coming year. It recommends the construction of seven additional unarmored steel cruisers, three of which should conform to the types already adopted, as represented by the Chicago, the Boston, and the Dolphin. Of the other four, two should be heavily armed cruising gunboats of about 1,500 tons displacement. These would be of the same size as

the Dolphin, but constructed on a different plan, because intended to supply a different want. In the
Dolphin, which is designed for a specific purpose,
actual fighting and working qualities are limited, so
as to obtain the maximum speed and endurance
possible with her size, while in the proposed vessels
the aim will be to secure the highest amount of
efficiency for general service, both in peace and war.
Finally, in view of the necessity for a certain number of vessels of small size and light draft, the
Board recommends the construction of two gunboats
of about 750 tons displacement, and not more than
nine feet draft, which shall be capable of going to sea
and also of navigating shallow waters.

"The estimated cost of vessels of the proposed
types is as follows :

Type.	Hull.	Machinery.	Ordnance.	Equipment.	Total.
Chicago..........	$650,000	$350,000	$225,000	$70,000	$1,295,000
Boston...........	450,000	260,000	168,000	58,000	936,000
Dolphin	232,000	175,000	50,000	25,000	482,000
Heavy gunboat...	216,000	175,000	100,000	25,600	516,000
Light gunboat....	132,000	77,000	40,000	20,000	269,000

"The total cost of the five vessels, one of each type,
will be $3,498,000, and adding the cost of the two
additional vessels of the last two types, the total
cost of the seven vessels proposed by the Board, and
aggregating 13,500 tons, will be $4,283,000.

"The Board expresses the opinion that the limit of
combined efficiency and economy is reached in the
cruiser of the Chicago type, of 4,500 tons displacement, and it condemns any policy looking to the
present construction of cruisers that shall rival in

speed the fastest transatlantic steamers. The mer-chant steamers having this exceptionally high speed comprise less than one-hundredth part of the ocean steam-tonnage of the world, either in number or value, and most of them in the event of a war would be withdrawn from their ordinary pursuits. In order to match their speed it would be necessary to build vessels with a displacement of at least 11,000 tons ; and while the great draft and dimensions of such vessels would confine their general efficiency within the narrowest limits, they would absorb for their maintenance and management an undue share of the current appropriations and of the existing allowance of seamen. Furthermore, the cost of building and fully equipping one such vessel would be at least $4,000,000, or nearly as much as that of all the seven ships recommended by the Board.

"In the above opinion and recommendations the Department concurs. If, however, it should appear to Congress desirable to construct one vessel in which all other qualities shall be sacrificed to the attainment of the highest possible speed, and to pro-vide for maintaining it in commission, the Depart-ment will gladly submit plans and estimates there-for, and the vessel when completed will no doubt add to the capabilities of the Navy. But the im-mediate object should be at moderate expense to re-place our worn-out cruisers with modern construc-tions fitted for general service, and for this reason the reconstruction should for the present be con-tinued on the lines already begun. In representing the recommendations of the Board, the Department, in addition, advises the construction of one of the

five steel rams recommended by the first Advisory
Board, November 7, 1881, and by the report of last
year; of one cruising torpedo-boat, at a cost of
$38,000, advocated by the same Board, and by the
present Board in its memorandum of November 21,
1882 ; and of two of the ten harbor torpedo-boats
recommended by the first Board, of the kind asked
for in the ordnance report of this year.

"The recommendations of the Board and the
Department are believed to be in pursuance of a
wise plan for that reconstruction of our naval force
which all admit is, in some form and to some extent,
indispensable to the national welfare. Such a plan
should conform to the demands of our national policy.
The scope of that policy, as it relates to the maintenance of a military establishment, has been clearly
and ably outlined by the late President Garfield, and
his judicious words may well serve as guides in any
action that we may take to-day. In a speech made
in 1878, in the House of Representatives, he said :
'The men who created this Constitution also set it
in operation, and developed their own idea of its
character. That idea was unlike any other that
then prevailed upon the earth. They made the
general welfare of the people the great source and
foundation of the common defence. In all nations
of the old world the public defence was provided for
by great standing armies, navies, and fortified posts,
so that the nation might every moment be fully
armed against danger from without or turbulence
within. Our fathers said : "Though we will use the
taxing power to maintain a small army and navy,
sufficient to keep alive the knowledge of war, yet

the main reliance for our defence shall be the intelligence, culture, and skill of our people ; a development of our own intellectual and material resources which will enable us to do everything that may be necessary to equip, clothe, and feed ourselves in time of war, and make ourselves intelligent, happy, and prosperous in peace." '

" With the views of American policy thus expressed the Department is in perfect accord. It is not now, and it never has been, a part of that policy to maintain a fleet able at any time to cope on equal terms with the foremost European armaments. The possibility of such war is not lost sight of ; but with our isolated position, and traditional peace policy, it is a remote contingency, and we should cherish no ambition to take the lead among the naval powers of the world ; certainly not until we again become foremost in the possession of a merchant marine. Any difference which would involve us in a conflict with one of the great powers should be the growth of time, affording opportunity for gradual preparation. On the other hand, in order to be prepared, not merely by the potentiality of our immense resources, but also by an actual armament, to assert at all times our natural, justifiable, and necessary ascendency in the affairs of the American hemisphere, we unquestionably need vessels in such numbers as fully to 'keep alive the knowledge of war,' and of such a kind that it shall be a knowledge of modern war ; capable on brief notice of being expanded into invincible squadrons. It is well known that we have not the elements of such a force to-day. The condition of decrepitude into which the fleet has fallen,

through a failure to provide for its gradual re-
newal by modern ships, is justly a subject of rid-
icule at home and abroad. The vessels available
for actual service are insufficient to give training to
the officers and seamen, unequal to the present
necessities of the Government, and unworthy of a
great and prosperous maritime state.

"The specific plan, which, in the opinion of the
Department, should be adopted, looks to a gradual
replacement of the present decaying fleet by modern
constructions. The proviso of the Act of March 3,
1883, limiting the repair of wooden ships to 20 per
cent. of their cost, should be continued in force, in
order that no money may be expended in rebuilding
wornout structures of an obsolete type. Provision
should then be made for building new cruisers, with
due care and economy, by an annual outlay extending over a considerable period. At least seven
modern vessels should be built in each year, until
the Government has acquired a new steel navy. Of
the annual expenditure of four millions which such
a plan would require, from one-third to one-half can
be saved by abandoning attempts to rebuild the
present wooden fleet, and by otherwise retrench-
ments in the naval appropriations.

" In pursuance of the act of Congress of August 5,
1882, and of reports of the inspection boards, made
as therein directed, the following condemned vessels
have been stricken from the Navy Register : Congress, Guard, Plymouth, Kansas, Emerald, Massachusetts, Sabine, Connecticut, Iowa, Niagara, Oregon,
Ohio, Pennsylvania, Virginia, Florida, Blue Light,
New Orleans, Colossus, Java, Susquehanna, Glance,

Burlington, Supply, Sorrel, Antietam, Dictator, Frolic, Relief, Pawnee, Rose, Benicia, Nyack, Saco, Old Monadnock, Narragansett, Tuscarora, Alaska, Worcester, Canandaigua, Jean Sands, Shawmut, Savannah, Santee, Phlox, Wyoming, Roanoke.

"Of these vessels, the Wyoming, Antietam, Supply, Emerald, Santee, Phlox, Jean Sands, and Rose have been reserved for purposes for which they can be made useful, or for future sale. The Massachusetts, Connecticut, Oregon, Pennsylvania, Virginia, Colossus, Java, and Canandaigua, all except the last being uncompleted at the navy yards, will doubtless be there taken to pieces, as they cannot be advantageously sold. The remaining twenty-seven vessels, excluding the Florida, Pawnee, and Benicia, for which no bids were made, have been sold to the highest bidders, in accordance with the statute. Their appraised value was $330,100, and they sold for $384,753, an advance of $54,653 over the appraisement.

"Sales at public auction of condemned stores and supplies have also been made at the navy yards under the provisions of the second section of the act, amounting to about $138,000." Wise words are these, and not the least pregnant of the most statesmanlike document ever issued by the Navy Department, and we should bear them in mind, for our naval future and national honor hinge upon their truth.

The first Advisory Board, in its report of November 7, 1881, gave an estimate of the required strength of a suitable unarmored cruising fleet. The report of this Board, composed of eminent naval officers, represents the highest professional opinion, and certainly these officers would not underestimate the necessities of the Government. The standard adopted by them may therefore be safely regarded as a maximum for the naval force in time of peace. The report fixed the number of vessels required in commission at all times at forty-three, and the reserve at twenty-seven, making a total of seventy. To provide such a force it recommended the construction of thirty-eight vessels. Further deterioration in the existing fleet since the report was made will necessitate an increase in the number of new ships in order to obtain the force established by the Board. As sufficient for that result, the Navy Department therefore advises the continuance of the policy recommended, of building annually at least seven new ships during the next ten years, before the end of which period the country will find itself possessed of a modern steel navy in every way adequate to the maintenance of the safety and honor of the nation.

CHAPTER X.

DURING the last session of Congress two notable reports upon the commercial marine were submitted, one by the Secretary of the Navy, the other by the joint committee appointed to investigate the causes of the decline of American shipping. Both agreed materially as to the means required for the revival of our merchant marine ; and there was an equal agreement as to the necessity of some centralized, logical form of administration. Upon this latter point Mr. Chandler said in his report : " The various services now charged with the supervision and regulation of matters relating to the merchant marine should be brought together in one department or bureau of the Government, which should be distinctly charged with the execution of laws concerning the shipping interests of the country, and to which ship owners could look for assistance and for the reception and presentation of their claims. There exists at present no responsible head to which are entrusted the interests of our merchant marine. Those branches of the subject of which the Government undertakes supervision are so scattered among subordinate officers, variously related, and loosely organized, that the industry might as well be left to itself." "The simplest and most natural method of

accomplishing the desired object," he continues,
"consists in the establishment of a Bureau of Mercantile Marine in the Navy Department.

The Congressional Committee at the conclusion
of its report declared, that "the English merchant
marine and English commerce have been greatly
aided by the watchful supervision and regulations of
the British Board of Trade, whose president is a
member of the Cabinet. In the executive department of our Government we have no board nor bureau with similar duties and power, and none which
is required by law even to keep a watchful eye over
the interests of our shipping, except for the purposes of collecting the revenues. Whether it would
not be wise to establish in the Treasury Department
a Bureau or Board of Commerce and Navigation, of
which the Secretary of the Treasury should be the
official head, with powers and duties in some respect
akin to those of the British Board of Trade, is already under consideration by the Committees on
Commerce of the Senate and the House, and will
undoubtedly receive the attention it deserves."

These suggested plans of administration differ only
in the departments to which they were to be entrusted, and in the degree of authority which it was
proposed to vest; both are excellent in principle,
because the tendency is in the right direction, and
from either only good can come. In considering the
question in the light of the failure of this bill, it becomes therefore a question simply how and where
the best results may be obtained.

The English Board of Trade is composed of "the
Lords of the Committee of the Privy Council ap-

pointed for the consideration of matters relating to
Trade and Foreign Plantations." Under the presi-
dency of a. member of the Cabinet, who is assisted
by a parliamentary and a permanent secretary, there
are five departments, viz. : Harbor, Marine, Railway,
Finance, and Statistical, each in charge of an assistant
secretary, and one, Law, under the direction of a
solicitor. Professional experts are attached to each,
naval officers serving on the Marine and Harbor
Boards, and military officers upon the Railway staff.
The general duties of the Board in relation to English vessels may be found in Part·I. of the "Merchant Shipping Acts." This code of laws is admirable in the breadth and wisdom of its provisions, and
so far as the conditions permit, it is enforced with
zeal and intelligence ; there are, however, objections
to the methods of administration, which would obtain equally here with the plan proposed by the
Congressional Committee. Broadly stated these are,
First, that the control is given to officials whose
fitness may be questioned because of their want
of the special training which is vital. *Secondly*, .that
an important and specific branch of government is
made a part of a general department, which administers enormous and most variant interests. *Thirdly*,
that though each of these interests is distinct in its
aims and purposes, and requires a special experience,
yet all are brought together in a system where the
final jurisdiction rests with officials who cannot
have either the sufficient knowledge or training
which the responsibility assumed presupposes ; and
Fourthly, that a new bureau is created while an old
one already exists which is not only co-central in its

purposes, but is in possession of such advantages for
the work that the control of the merchant marine
will not involve its own affairs with those of any
other branch of Government.

These are the general objections to the system
recommended by the Congressional Committee ; but
there are others governed by political considerations.
For those who desire more detailed information as
to the defects of our present laws, including a comparison of our system with that of other countries,
and a full argument as to the establishment of a
central bureau in the Navy Department, the Appendices to the Report of the Secretary of the Navy for
last year are open.

No two branches of government are more nearly
allied than the navy and the merchant marine.   The
first responsibility of a naval establishment is the defence of a nation's coast, this being the pure and simple duty of men who transfer destructive energy from
shore to sea; and its second is the guardianship of a
nation's commerce afloat.   In return the merchant
marine is the school where the reserve which may
be called into action during emergencies or war is
trained and maintained.   If there were no merchant
marine there would be no need for a navy either to
foster commerce or to police and survey the seas,
and a naval establishment would consist very properly of coast-defence vessels manned by stokers, and
by such artillerymen as had their sea-legs.   But a
merchant marine is an economical necessity to every
sea-board country ; for, briefly generalized, its advantages are that it enriches in seasons of general
peace the nations owning it, and instils that sense

of self-respect which comes from healthy rivalry with other competing maritime countries ; when neutral nations are at war it secures the safe transmission of property belonging to its citizens, and relieves them from a perilous dependence upon the ships of nations liable to capture and confiscation ; in war or when an emergency arises, it becomes the reserve from which seamen and officers are to be drawn ; and at all times it advances prosperity at home, and promotes and diffuses the influence of a nation beyond its borders far more than agriculture, mines, or manufactures. It quickens a nation's powers and infuses life and vigor into its international relations ; for the flag flying at the mast-head of a vessel typifies the individuality of a country and asserts its place among the governments of the world. The merchant marine, therefore, claims protection in its best and widest sense abroad and at home; and in the high seas and in foreign waters this means safety from alien interference by capture, destruction, detention, search, or insult. To afford protection effective war ships and competent crews are necessary ; the first must always be the best which the modern idea can design; they must be sufficient in number to show the flag everywhere, and they must have such means of offence and defence as to impress an enemy, whether open or disguised, with the necessity of fair play. A competent personnel implies good men and trained officers and so many of both that duty afloat and ashore may be performed with efficiency and fidelity ; and finally there must be an active reserve from which reliefs can be drawn at all times, and a po-

tential one which in emergencies will supply the
trained seamen upon whom the safety of the country
mainly depends.   Therefore is it that the obligations
of the merchant marine and the navy are mutual
and interdependent so far as they relate to the defence of a country in war and to the protection of
commercial interests in foreign waters under all circumstances.

At home there is a relationship no less close.
Under any proper system the administration of the
shipping of a nation requires educated officials,
specially trained in maritime affairs ; the national
safety depends upon the maintenance and instruction at all times of a reasonable naval force ; there
must be a nucleus of war ships, of sailors, and of
officers ; not so many of these, it is true, as the possibilities of attack demand, but more than the operations of peace require ; that is, there must be enough
to meet the first necessities of those emergencies
which always arise.   There is no escape from this
simple proposition, and hence, being obliged to keep
such a force, the nation can be best and most economically served by extending the sphere of active
naval employment so as to require officers and seamen of the navy to perform all the work of the
national government upon or in direct connection
with the ocean.   "This clear and salutary principle," writes Mr. Chandler, "should be deliberately
adopted and effectually enforced in all proper methods by the national Congress," for its outcome would
be to invigorate, improve, and strengthen the navy
"not only without increased expense to the Government, but with results of positive economy."   Its

effect upon the merchant marine can be best made
plain by a statement of the necessities of this latter
service.

Under every form of government shipping is entitled to the same treatment and care as any other
form of invested capital. That their titles may be
clear, vessels are enrolled, registered, and licensed ;
and their fitness for the trusts reposed in them is
guaranteed by their survey, measurement, and inspection. Besides these precautions it is the duty of the
State to see that reasonable security against accidents is assured ; that crews and officers are properly
selected, and that their rights and those of passengers, shippers, insurers, and owners are guarded ; that
the health of all seafaring persons is not endangered by the parsimony, indifference or cruelty of
ship-owners or of persons in immediate authority on
shipboard ; and that in case of illness or disability,
humane and skilful treatment is provided. The high
seas passed over, the coasts approached, and the
harbors entered should be freed from those dangers which science can remove or, failing that, these
should be so clearly distinguished as to minimize all
chances of accident ; robberies, piracies, and general
crimes should be detected and punished ; and, in the
event of casualties, permanent and ample provision
should be made for the safety of the lives and of
the cargoes thus imperilled. All these details may
be grouped in three classes : *First*, those which apply to merchant vessels only, viz., the enrolment,
registry, and license of vessels and their inspection,
measurement, and survey ; the examination and engagement of officers and the shipment and certifica-

tion of seamen ; and the preservation of the health of crews afloat. *Secondly*, those which affect equally merchant and naval shipping, viz., the survey of oceans, coasts, harbors, and inland navigable waters ; the service of light-houses, light-ships, beacons, and buoys ; the general laws governing pilotage ; and the life-saving service. *Thirdly*, that one condition which is purely naval in its demands, viz., the police of the high seas and of tide and inland waters.

These duties are strictly maritime ; in two of the classes the demands of naval administration are clearly evident ; and in the remaining one the beneficial effects of similar control are no less potent. At present the enrolment, registry, and license of vessels belong to the Register of the Treasury, with the regular work of whose office they have no connection save that arising from the fact that such an official may be a properly constituted person to register everything from bonds to barnacles ; with equal propriety, however, it might be assumed that the duty would fall within the province of an election bureau, because it enrolls voters, or be entrusted to the mayor's deputy because he licenses dogs for the summer months. The inspection of steam vessels also draws its inspiration from one of the heads of the Treasury Hydra, why, no one seems clearly to know. This inspection service consists of a supervising inspector general ; of supervising inspectors ; of inspectors of foreign vessels, and of local inspectors. It is more or less abused as a very close corporation, and is said by competent authority to further the interests entrusted to it by a star-chamber process, which culminates in its reporting to

and legislating for itself. Each district has a number of local boards made up of an inspector of
hulls and an inspector of boilers. The former is
required to satisfy himself as to the structure of
ships, the accommodations for passengers and crew,·
the completeness of equipment for saving life and
for extinguishing fire, and the sufficiency of anchors
and cables. The latter must inquire into the safety of
boilers and engines, including everything which per-
tains to steam machinery. Acting as a board, the
two inspectors examine the qualifications of masters,
chief mates, engineers and pilots of steam vessels,
and upon their favorable report licenses for the
term of one year are issued. They receive from licensed officers the reports of all accidents, and they
investigate charges of incompetency or of neglect
against such officers, having power to summon wit-
nesses and, upon proof of misbehavior, negligence, or
unskilfulness, to suspend or revoke licenses. These
are very important duties and require special qualifications—to determine which there is a board consisting of a supervising inspector, a *collector of customs* and—a DISTRICT JUDGE.

The shipping of seamen is under the direction of
commissioners whose duties are prescribed in the
statutes of the country. It is a matter of record
that these officials, even with the best intentions, are
unable to overcome the difficulties which beset their
duties. So far as any guarantees of capacity go, the
crews of· all vessels and the officers serving in any
sea-going craft, except in steamers, are without the
least control. Marine Insurance Companies and the
American Ship Masters' Association of the Port of

New York have endeavored to correct the lack of
training and experience in officers by providing lim-
itations, but unavailingly ; and to-day the lives and
cargoes of our citizens are entrusted to pseudo-ma-
riners whose qualifications rest upon their relationship to the master, owner, or other interested person.
No examinations are required, and we are forced to
trust our lives and property to so many incompe-
tent merchant officers, because of our theory that
the interests of an owner are so important that he
will not submit them to any risk.   But this covers
neither the insurer nor the passenger, and the melancholy roll of American wrecks proves upon what an
unstable foundation this claim rests. The control of
the commissioners over the seamen is only less than
that of the Government over these officials themselves,
for they are not directly connected with any executive
department, and are appointed by those hardy tars
and expert mariners—*the Judges of the Circuit Court.*

The organization for the care of sick and disabled
seamen, with its numerous and spacious hospitals,
and its large corps of surgeons, is known as the Marine Hospital Service, and is in charge of a bureau
of the Treasury Department ; it is supported chiefly
by a monthly tax of forty cents on the wages of all
seamen, and is administered by surgeons whose appointments come from the Secretary of the Treasury.
Naval seamen are cared for by another department
and by a separate corps of practitioners, who pass
competitive examinations for their positions ; in
some places there are duplicate hospitals, marine and
naval, usually large buildings intended for the maximum demands which war or pestilence may make ;

in one instance, at least, two of these edifices occupy
adjoining grounds, and with a divided duty, and
more or less deprecation of each other's usefulness,
stare one another out of countenance—vacantly.
Sea Hygiene has a place, and an important one, in
the modern scientific world, and notable and most
useful contributions have been made to it by our
naval officers. The excellent sanitary conditions of
men-of-war at this date are due to the intelligent
study and zeal of our surgeons, and nowhere are
there officials better qualified to bring the standard of
merchant ships to the plane which our civilization
demands. Their appreciation of the physical needs
of seafaring people has been gained on shipboard,
and though their fight against wet decks, insufficient and badly cooked food and defective ventilation
has been a bitter one, yet the victory happily is with
them now. It is generally believed that the sphere
of experience of the surgeons of the Marine Hospital
Service is, perforce of circumstances, a limited one,
and that like our naval constructors, they have never
studied that special part of their profession which
their appointments require, in the only place where it
can be properly learned—at sea with a sailor *clientelle*.

All these duties are maritime, and should be gathered and welded together in order that they may acquire coherency and efficiency. The control should
be given to a central department, maritime in its
character ; and for its special administration a Bureau
of Maritime Marine should be created, relegating
the Marine Hospital Service to the care of the Naval
Bureau of Medicine and Surgery. Congressional
action should then take this form : *First*, the trans-

fer to the Navy Department of all the duties in relation to the registry, enrolment and license of vessels, the regulation of steam vessels, and the shipment of seamen. *Secondly*, the creation of a Bureau
of Mercantile Marine which shall administer the
above ; and, *Thirdly*, the passage of a general law
as similar to the British Merchant Act as the differences of our institutions and the requirement of the
foregoing provisions will admit. House Bill No.
7158 (1883) provided for the first two of these. The
general control was given to the Secretary of the
Navy, who was to be assisted by a board to be known
as the Mercantile Marine Board, and to be composed of the following persons : The chief of the
Bureau of Mercantile Marine and the supervising
inspector general of steamboats, *ex officio ;* five civilians to be appointed by the President, among whom
there were to be one experienced seaman and navigator, one shipbuilder, skilled in designing and constructing vessels of wood and iron, one scientific
man of eminent attainments, and two persons of special experience in commercial and maritime affairs ;
and finally three officers of the navy, likewise to be
appointed by the President, one of whom was to be
a naval constructor, one a chief engineer, and one a
line officer, the last named to act as secretary of the
Board. Sections 11 and 12 prescribed the duties of
this Board as follows : To consider and investigate the
condition of the mercantile marine, and to advise and
assist the Secretary of the Navy in making rules and
regulations for executing the laws in relation to it ;
and to report the results of its investigations to Congress. Section 3 established the Bureau of Mercantile

Marine and entrusted it with the various duties enumerated before ; contracting them in some particulars and amplifying them in others.   One notable change was the appointment of an additional inspector of vessels, who was to report upon the strength and sufficiency of the equipment, and the completeness and efficiency of the navigating instruments and charts ; and to examine into the fitness of master, mate, or pilot of any vessel.   In addition to the duties already defined, the Bureau was to have charge of the regulations governing the safety of ships and the prevention of accidents ; the draught of water and the location of load water lines ; the heights of freeboard ; the running lights, the fog-signals, and the rules of the road at sea ; the provisions, health, and accommodations of passengers and crews ; the protection of seamen from impositions ; the misconduct of passengers ; and all inquiries into wrecks, casualties, and salvage.   A Registrar General of Seamen was to compile and preserve all records relating to the qualifications and service of officers, seamen, and apprentices, and to provide for examinations, for the granting of certificates, and for the making of apprenticeships.   In order to carry out the details of the Bureau it was proposed that Local Marine Offices should be established, where should be kept the records of sales, transfers, and hypothecations of vessels ; seamen were to be shipped and discharged there, as in England, without any charge ; and the local boards of inspection were to keep their records and to hold their investigations, and all officers were to be examined in the same place.   In brief, these offices, in every shipping town of any size, were to be to the sailor and the ship-owner what the custom-house is, or ought to be, to the merchant and broker.

Few words are necessary to show the advantages which would accrue from the transfer to the Navy Department of the duties grouped above in the second class as partly naval and partly mercantile. At present the Coast Survey is nominally a bureau in the Treasury Department. "Its primary object, as expressed in the Statute (Revised Statutes, Section 4681), is to cause a survey to be taken of the coasts of the United States, in which shall be designated the islands and shoals, with the roads or places of anchorage, within twenty leagues of any part of the shores of the United States." Subsequent legislation extended its operations to parts of the ocean beyond the original limit, and provided for deep-sea soundings, current observations, and for a hydrographic development of the dangers of ocean navigation on the west coast of North America. There are, at present, eleven vessels in commission in this service, eight on the Atlantic and Gulf coasts, and three on the Pacific coast ; six of these are steamers and the remainder are schooners. In this service sixty-one naval officers and two hundred and seventy-five seamen are employed, continuing that policy which for fifty years has given the hydrography of our coast to the trained officers of the navy ; of the officers now on the active list two hundred and thirty-two have been on the survey at different times and with excellent results to both. Marine surveying, and the preparation and distribution of charts and sailing directions, are duties which naturally fall within the scope of a naval establishment, and to-

day not only is the Hydrographic Office of the
Naval Bureau of Navigation exercising these functions, but the actual work on the coast is performed
by naval officers, and one-third of the total cost of
the whole survey is borne by naval appropriations.
Its connection with the Treasury is of the most remote character, and no good reason can be given for
a separation of duty and authority which would be
mutually enhanced by consolidation.   In any event
its present position is an anomaly; for if topographi-
cal work be the main duty, this should be relegated
to a bureau of the Interior Department, which should
have general charge of all surveys on land; while
the sea and coast work proper should be placed
under the direct control of the Hydrographic Office
of the Navy.   Our surveys are admirable in character, but are entrusted to no less than four different
Departments of the General Government, the operations of which are continually overlapping. A broad
generalization would give all topography to the Department of the Interior, and all hydrography to
that of the Navy.   This would abolish the Coast
Survey in its present form, and limit Army duty to
its legitimate sphere, and with the advantage of con-
solidating the work to be done.

The Light-House Board has charge not only of
light-houses, but of the establishment and care of
all other aids to navigation—light-ships, beacons,
buoys, fog-signals, and sea marks.   It is under the
Treasury Department, and is administered by a
board of nine members : three officers of the navy,
three officers of the corps of engineers of the army,
and three civilians, one of whom must be the Secre-

tary of the Treasury, and the remaining two persons of high scientific attainments. Its original assignment is explained by the fact that at that time the Navy Department did not exist. For some years it was under the superintendence of the Commissioner of the Revenue, and afterward of the Fifth Auditor, but the defects of both plans led to the formation, mainly through the exertions of naval officers, of the present Board. There are fourteen light-house districts : six on the Atlantic, two on the Gulf, and four on the Pacific coast; along the Great Lakes there are two ; and there is one on the Ohio River, and one which extends from the head of navigation of the Mississippi and of the Missouri to New Orleans. The report for 1883 shows that the Government owns :

Light-houses.. 723
Light-ships... 30
Fog-signals operated by steam or hot air.................. 64
Fog-bells operated by machinery.......................... 115
Beacon lights on Western rivers.......................... 860
Day or unlighted beacons 345
Automatic whistling buoys................................ 33
Automatic bell-buoys 14
Other buoys...3,377
Steam tenders... 22
Steam launches.. 4
Sailing tenders... 2
Light keepers, including laborers, in charge of Western river
    lights...1,769
Other employes, including crews of light-ships and tenders.. 686
    The appropriations for the fiscal year, were :
For the establishment............................... $2,249,000
For light-houses, fog-signals, etc.................. 500,000

        Total.. $2,749,000

These lights are divided into seven classes, with an intermediate class between the third and fourth, and two others known as lantern and lens divisions. Each district is under the personal charge and super-intendence of a naval officer, detailed exclusively for this duty; in three of the districts there are also naval officers employed as assistants ; and three more are members of the Board in Washington, one of these being chairman and the other naval secretary. The army officers, apart from those on the Board, have supervision only of the erection and repair of build-ings and apparatus, most of this being performed incidentally and in addition to their regular duties under the War Department. As this service is alto-gether maritime in its character, and so largely naval in its administration, there seems no reason why its transfer should not be made to the Navy Department.

The statutes of the United States authorize the several States to make their own pilotage laws, the general government surrendering nearly all of its supervising power. In Maine and New Hampshire pilots are appointed by the Governor and Council upon the recommendation of the ship-owners and ship-masters of any port. In Massachusetts, commis-sioners license them, except for the ports of Boston and New Bedford, where the power of appointment rests finally with the Governor. In the port of New York, two boards have concurrent jurisdiction, one known as the Board of Commissioners of Pilot-age, and consisting of three commissioners chosen by the Chamber of Commerce and two by the Board of Underwriters of the City of New York ; and the other

made up of seven commissioners appointed by the
Governor of New Jersey with the advice and consent
of the State Senate ; each of these boards has power
to license its own pilots and is given all authority
over them. In Pennsylvania, pilots are selected by a
board of wardens ; in Maryland, by an examining
board, and in Alabama and Louisiana, by the harbor
masters and port wardens. These plans are practically the same, and there are no objections to them under
our theory of government, but some general jurisdiction over pilotage boards should belong to the
nation. Salutary laws, looking to the interests of
all classes of citizens, should be passed. Compulsory pilotage should be kept within those proper
limits which, while not unduly burdening owners
and shippers, protect the lives of passengers and
crews, and supply the incentive for zeal, courage,
and sacrifice upon the part of the pilots. All fees
ought to be based upon a reasonable law which gives
adequate compensation for the risks assumed, and
does not create a crushing monopoly that drives shipping from our ports. Masters and mates who can
pass the proper examinations should receive pilot certificates, granted upon conditions which can be easily
formulated, and each district should be compelled to
make returns of the regulations and ordinances under which it works, including a full description of
its pilots and apprentices, with the character of the
services for which each is licensed, the rates of pilotage in force, and the total amount of money received—in this last distinguishing between the
charges upon American and foreign ships, respectively. Nothing of this is mentioned in the Report

of the Secrétary, but it seems a part of the general
plan, and would naturally be entrusted to the Navigation Bureau of the Navy Department. The Life-
saving Service is under the direction of a bureau in
the Treasury Department, and as its general duties
are administered by officers of the Revenue Marine,
the reasons for its transfer will follow those affecting
that service.

The third class of the general group is that which
performs duties purely naval, viz., the police of the
high seas and of tide and inland waters. This is the
province of the Navy and of the Revenue Marine.
The last named service is controlled by a Treasury
Bureau, and requires, to maintain its efficiency, 185
officers and 36 vessels; 23 of the latter are sea-
going steamers, fifteen being propellers varying from
131 to 403 tons, and eight paddlers varying from
201 to 499 tons. Its working limits are harbor and
coast cruising, and in addition to preventing infrac-
tions of customs laws, assisting in collecting the
revenue, and aiding distressed vessels, it performs
those duties of police along the coast which the navy
exercises on the high seas and in foreign waters.
The crews are armed; the cutters carry from one to
four guns, and in war are always pressed into the
naval service. The present separation is an absur-
dity, and by the proposed transfer to the Navy Department mutual benefit will result. The Revenue
Marine will gain in every way, by its connection
with a department which is administering maritime affairs on a large plan and is looking, not to
the personal aggrandizement of a few officials, but
to the best interests of the Government; it will de-

rive all the benefits which enhanced experience, intelligence, and zeal can yield ; the standard of its officers will be raised by the discipline and routine enforced through naval methods ; and their possibilities of usefulness will be increased by making them a part of a permanent body in which their commissions will be insured against the operations either of malice or of favoritism, and their services will be rewarded by dignified offices of retirement at an age when duty well done deserves the graceful recognition of a grateful country.

The transfer will benefit the navy by opening to its junior officers a new school of experience which will thus inure them to the dangers and teach them the necessities of our coast at their most plastic age mentally, and when their resources physically, actual and in reserve, are greatest ; it will give them that familiarity with the coast and harbors which is so essential in war and peace ; and thus increase their maritime usefulness by making them better surveyors and light-house inspectors of the future ; finally, it will give them practice in handling vessels of the smallest sizes under difficult circumstances, and provide in every way a field of training which will make them better naval officers.

It utilizes for the country a personnel that must be kept at a high standard, and economically and most efficiently employs the services of officers in a sphere which by their training they are in every way qualified to occupy—and this under a general control which is the life of all organization. The transfer would not interfere in any way with the present officers of the Revenue Marine, for they

would retain their duties until in the course of years
a policy of absorption resulted in making the service
wholly naval. Under the provisions of the bill introduced last year, no officer in the Revenue Marine
could ever be placed under the command of a naval
officer, nor be ranked in his present sphere of duties
by any such person; for it was explicitly guaranteed
that vacancies in the upper grades were to be filled by
promotion from the lower grades in the corps, and
that naval officers could be detailed for duty only as
vacancies were made at the bottom of the list. To
harmonize all the interests it was proposed to transfer the service to the Navy; the small vessels employed in harbors to belong to the Treasury, and the
larger ones to be assigned to duty, as at present,
upon the requisition of the Secretary of the Treasury, their movements in each district being directed
for the time being by the collector of customs.

The result of all these changes would have been the
creation of two new bureaus in the Navy Department, the amplification of the duties of two bureaus
already existing, and the passage of a general act
based upon the necessities of our shipping. Opposition was evoked, mainly by small bodies of interested
officials, though, to some degree also, by the ignorance of our citizens in regard to the questions at
issue,—and the measure failed. But dispassionate
examination will do much to correct this, and will
show the necessity of the reforms proposed and of
immediate action; for the demands formulated here
are founded upon justice and intelligence, and are
for the general good of the whole country.

CHAPTER XI.

IF the arguments advanced in the preceding pages are correct, the restoration of our merchant marine, its efficient conduct, and its central administration are matters mainly of intelligent legislation. Apart from special beliefs, it seems but fair to assume that all who have examined the subject concede that these things should be done. This being granted, nothing remains but to recapitulate the facts already set forth, in order to emphasize the reasons why it is believed that the special plan proposed in this book should be adopted.

Briefly, then, it seems to be certain that ships are profitable abroad, and can be made profitable here. We were a great maritime people and, by the position we assumed, proved incontestably that of all competing nations we possessed most fully those qualities essential to maritime success, viz., national instinct, and necessities of environment in land population and geographical position. Our commerce had gone to the very fore-front of man's adventure on the high seas ; then paused, retreated, and finally almost perished. This decadence, however, was not due, as is generally claimed, to the war between the States in 1861, to the revival of a general prosperity which left no money for investment in shipping, to the

fluctuations of an unstable currency, or to that unholy trinity of British gold, a hireling press, and a
foreign insurance ring which so vexes certain doctrinaires ; but had its origin, purely, in those changes
which commerce theories demanded, and which we
failed to adopt, videlicet, the substitution of steam
for sail, the use of iron in place of wood for ship-
building, the antiquated navigation laws of this
country, and the burdensome National and State
taxes.

Subsidies will not correct these evils, for they have
been tried and found wanting, and the great foreign
trades have been established not by a grant of public
money to a favored few, but by the liberalization of
the world's commerce to the bold essay of free men
in free ships. To regain our position, to hope even
for a share of our legitimate carrying trade, we must
in the beginning adopt certain measures of reform.
These are : *First*, the admission to American register of all ships over 3,000 tons, subject to the same
laws regarding ownership which now prevail, save in
one or two important particulars. *Secondly*, the admission duty free of all materials to be used in the
construction and repair of vessels of over 3,000 tons.
Thirdly, the adoption of new tonnage measurements,
based on actual carrying capacity, and excluding the
space occupied by engines and boilers, and accommodations for officers and crew. *Fourthly*, exemption from taxation, local and national, on all vessels
engaged in the foreign trade for more than eight
months of the year. *Fifthly*, permission for all American vessels in the foreign trade to take their stores
and shipchandlery out of bond duty free. *Sixthly*,

a general revision of the laws relating to seamen and the consular service. *Seventhly*, individual liability as to ownership. *Eighthly*, a general and equitable postal bill, with fair compensation for carrying the mails ; and, *Ninthly*, a change in the pilot laws— modifying compulsory pilotage and permitting masters and mates, when properly qualified, to pilot their own vessels.

Owning a profitable trade and free ships, we must manage it with a good personnel, for ignorance, carelessness, or dishonesty are the most fruitful sources of marine disasters. The percentage of American wreckages is greater than that of any other nation, and we must expect to maintain that proud eminence as long as we are absolutely without any guarantees as to the capacity of our foreign-going and home seafaring people. France, Italy, Russia, the North Countries, and Great Britain, all have plans of some kind ; but none of these seems so well suited to our necessities, nor so little antagonistic to our national genius and instinct, as that of England. It is practical enough not to hamper individual effort, and yet so theoretical that the mere rule-of-thumb mariner cannot, as he should not, be entrusted with interests which, humanly and commercially considered, are of enormous magnitude. There are examinations for officers and certifications for seamen, and the whole conduct of merchant shipping is controlled by a wise and general law. To supply the annual losses of the merchant marine there must be various sources of supply, one of which, at least, should be a nucleus of intelligence around which the brawn and muscle can rally. To give this training there are in

England nineteen ships, seventeen for seamen and two for officers, and, theorists to the contrary, the annual entrance into service afloat of the pupils of these schools has resulted in most pronounced good. Starting out fairly on a commercial enterprise, well found, well manned, and insured against unjust discriminations at home and abroad, vessels must have protection from foreign enemies and rivals. Hence there must be war ships to watch the commercial interests of a country. The first duty of a navy is the defence of its coasts at home, and of its citizens abroad ; the next is the protection of its commerce; and the third is the police and survey of its own shores and of the high seas in the general cause of humanity. But the economical demands of our country forbid the navy being maintained at a war standard, hence there must be a reserve of ships and of men from which aid can be drawn. A revived commerce means a revived and effective ship-building plant, and a large merchant marine supplies that potential reserve, upon which the integrity of the country, so far as sea defences go, mainly depends.

Finally, to administer all these various relations there must be a central bureau. Ships must ever carry the declaration of some national supervision over them, both as a protection to the owners as well as a warning to foreigners. They must have the imprimatur of some State that they are worthy the hire of those who seek transportation for themselves or for their goods upon the high seas ; and they must be forced, for the general welfare of the nation, at least, to carry competent crews and to guard the health of all who manage or sail in them.

11

These duties are maritime, and should be entrusted to some bureau or department which shares this distinctive character with them. There seems no question but that to the Navy Department these functions should be relegated, not only for reasons of special efficiency, but for those of economy. In the annual report for 1883 the Secretary of the Navy reasserts the reasons given in 1882 for the centralization and control of the national work upon the ocean.

"In the report from this Department of last year," he writes, "it was affirmed as a broad and salutary principle of administration, that the officers and seamen of the Navy should be employed to perform all the work of the national Government upon or in direct connection with the ocean. It was shown that such an extension of the field of naval employment would strengthen and invigorate the service without any detriment to existing interests, while the fusion of all branches of nautical administration would secure concentration of purpose, unity of action, and broader and more substantial results.

"The reasoning upon which this proposition is based is simple and obvious. The United States have an ocean commerce of 2,500,000 tons and a seacoast of 10,000 miles. Though the carrying trade has fallen largely into foreign hands, yet in maritime tonnage our country is still the second, and in extent of coast-line the third, in the world. Upon our coast lie more than twenty great cities, the centres of distribution for the products of the interior. What affects them affects the whole country. The only

safeguard for these important and vulnerable interests lies in the Navy. To dispense with a navy would
be to invite aggression and to insure disaster.

"The Navy, as an arm of maritime defence, is therefore a national necessity. It must be maintained
continuously for two purposes: to avert war, by
making it costly and dangerous for an opponent;
and to wage war, when it cannot be averted. From
the nature of things, however, the fulfilment of these
purposes cannot of itself give the naval force full and
continuous employment. Nevertheless, it must be
maintained, and maintained in a state of efficiency.
Although the contingency that will call it into full
activity is remote, its officers must always be kept in
readiness. If they cannot be, it would be better, for
the country's interest as well as for their own, that
they should be disbanded.

"There is only one way in which the people can
assure themselves that their Navy shall be always
thus prepared for service. It must be constantly
occupied to the full measure of its capacity; its occupations must be directly in the line of its profession; and they must be carried on under the supervision of that Department which is responsible for
its efficiency and discipline. If it were necessary, in
order to effect this, that new work should be devised
for the Navy to do, the result would be sufficiently
important to warrant the undertaking. But it is not
necessary. The Government is to-day performing,
by means of other officials and other establishments,
work which, in its general professional character and
in the professional training required, is indistinguish-
able from that of the Navy itself. A sound policy

demands that in it the Navy should be utilized, occupied, and practised.

"This nautical work now carried on by the Government outside of the Navy Department comprises the
surveying and lighting of the coast and its adjacent
islands ; the prohibition of illicit trade, the assistance
of vessels in distress, and the rescue of life and property from the perils of the sea ; the inspection of
the hulls and boilers of merchant steamers, with a
view to their safe navigation ; and the admeasurement and registration of vessels and the shipment and
care of seamen of the merchant marine.　The measures proposed by the Department consisted in the
application to this unquestionably nautical work of
the general principle advocated, and in its extension
in the same direction by an organized and practical
effort to supervise and advance the interests of our
decayed merchant marine.

"In applying the general principle to the nautical
work within the province of the Government, it is
found that one portion, the supervision of commerce
by a single branch of the executive, though highly
important and desirable, is not in operation at all ;
that a second portion, the shipment of seamen, is
carried on by subordinate officials under no executive supervision ; that a third portion, the surveying and lighting of the coast, is done almost wholly
by officers of the Navy, under the direction of the
Treasury Department ; while a fourth portion, consisting of the cutter service, the life-saving service,
and the steamboat inspection, is also committed to
bureaus in that Department, and is performed by
officials connected therewith.　In reference to the

supervision of commerce and the shipment of seamen, the question whether they shall be directed by
any Department, and, if so, by that of the Navy, is
one that may be determined on its merits, without
regard to existing relations. In reference to the
Coast Survey, it is clear that the present arrangement, by which the direction and control of a large
body of naval officers and seamen are transferred to
the Treasury Department, is unsuitable, unnecessary,
and detrimental to the interests of the Government.
As to the rest of the work, which is now wholly carried on by the same Department, while no criticism
is made upon the integrity or efficiency of its administration in any particular under the system adopted,
yet the expediency of the system itself becomes a
general question of national policy, which, not alone
in its bearing upon the useful employment of the
Navy, the Navy Department is competent and is
called upon to consider.

"In pursuance of this duty, and after careful inquiry and mature reflection, the Department, in its
report of last year, recommended that the Navy
should be employed, as far as was possible, to perform all this maritime work ; and it suggested a process by which the transfer might be accomplished
without any interruption of the operations of the
Government. The views then expressed have only
increased in strength, as added experience and discussion have thrown new light upon them. The
main points of the argument are therefore restated,
and the recommendations are emphatically renewed.

"The Light-House administration, charged with
the establishment and care of aids to navigation,

including light-houses, light-ships, beacons, buoys, fog-signals and sea-marks, performs a work under the Treasury Department which is strictly nautical in character; of which no one but a practical navigator is a competent judge; which requires a kind of skill and experience that the Navy alone can furnish; and all the essential parts of which, excepting only the erection and repair of buildings and apparatus, are carried on at this time by naval officers. Being nautical and not fiscal operations, they should be supervised by the Navy and not the Treasury Department.

"The Coast Survey, originally established for the purpose of making hydrographic charts, has of late years extended its functions in a totally different direction, that of geodetic surveys in the interior. In making this extension, it has gradually abandoned the water survey to the Navy, until how the actual work in this field is done almost exclusively by naval officers withdrawn for the purpose from the direction and control of their own Department. By an extraordinary anomaly in legislation, the United States Hydrographic Office, an indispensable branch of this Department, is allowed to survey and make charts of every coast in the world but that of the United States; while the best naval surveyors are claimed by another Department to perform this work under its supervision. Sixty-seven naval officers are now diverted in this manner from the direction of the Navy; and 280 seamen, out of the 7,500 allowed to the Navy, are now on board Coast Survey vessels.

"For such an arrangement there might be some

show of reason if the work upon which the officers
are engaged were specially connected with the
Department under which they are placed, and remote from the subjects of which their own Department has cognizance; but, in view of the fact that
no part of this work has the faintest traceable connection with the general purposes of the Treasury,
that its effectual performance is of vital importance
to the Navy, and that an office exists to-day in the
Navy Department where similar work is necessarily
carried on, it is inconceivable why so inconvenient,
artificial, and indefensible an arrangement should be
perpetuated.   The existing office might properly
continue the geodetic work, which seems gradually
to be absorbing its attention and its appropriations,
while the hydrographic surveys on our coast, now
performed by naval officers, under a naval inspector,
in the office of the Geodetic Survey, should be carried on, like other hydrographic surveys, by the
Naval Hydrographic Office.

"The duties of the Revenue Marine, as officially
defined, consist in cruising for the prevention of
illicit trade, and for the enforcement of certain laws
applicable to shipping, particularly those requiring
the registry, enrollment, and license of vessels, com-
pelling life-saving appliances to be kept therein, the
name and hailing port to be affixed, and lights to be
exhibited; prohibiting the overloading of passenger
ships, assessing the Marine-Hospital tax, and aiding
in the quarantine service of the States.   The cutters
further assist in enforcing the neutrality laws, and
those for the suppression of piracy, and for the protection of the timber reserves.   They are also called

upon to prevent unlawful traffic in rum and fire-arms in Alaska ; to protect the seal-fisheries, to suppress mutinies, and extinguish fires on board merchant-vessels, and to carry out the laws in aid of distressed seamen.

" Several of these duties, such as the enforcement of the neutrality laws, the suppression of piracy, of mutinies on board merchant-vessels, and the like, the ships of the navy are now charged with, and actually perform in common with revenue vessels. Of the rest, there is not one that is foreign to the general purpose and scope of the naval officer's profession. The only duty connected directly with the customs is that of the seizure of smugglers—a duty which is precisely similar to the naval officer's duty of searching and seizing, during war, vessels engaged in contraband trade. It requires a knowledge of the statutes relating to the subject, a knowledge not very difficult to acquire ; but beyond this nothing that is outside of a naval officer's necessary training. The duties of both services are identical in their general nature, only they operate in different localities. Both cruise to protect the maritime interests of the Government, and to render assistance to American vessels—the one on the coast, the other, in addition, at sea and in foreign waters. One polices the shore, the other the ocean. In war both engage in naval operations.

"The practical identity in the character of the Naval and the Revenue Marine Services lies in the fact that they are both nautical and both military. That the Revenue Marine is a nautical service requires no proof. It is nothing if not nautical. That

it is a military service was officially asserted by the
Treasury Department in the report on the service
for 1881, in these words :

" ' The Revenue Marine, while charged by law with
the performance of important civil duties, is essen-
tially military in its character.   Each vessel is provided with great guns, and furnished with as full a
complement of small arms for its crew as any ship
of war.   Its officers are required to be proficient in
military drill, and possess a thorough knowledge of
the uses of both great and small arms.   Its crews
are required to be instructed from day to day at the
great guns and in the use of the carbine, pistol, and
cutlass.   Commanding officers are required, while
boarding vessels arriving in ports of the United
States, in case of the failure or refusal of any such
vessel, on being hailed, to come to and submit to
the proper inspection by an officer of the service, to
fire, first across her bows as a warning, and, in case
of persistent refusal, to resort to shot or shell to
compel obedience.   In the performance of this
work, they are likely at any time to receive injuries,
and be subjected to the same dangers in time of
peace as the force employed on naval vessels.

" ' By the Act of March 2, 1799, it is provided that
" the revenue cutters shall, whenever the President
so directs, co-operate with the Navy."   It will be ob-
served that the co-operation of the two services prescribed in the act above quoted is not contingent
upon a state of war or other particularly perilous
conditions.   On the contrary, it may take place in
time of peace and for pacific purposes, and when
less hazard is involved to the two services than per-

tains to the discharge by a revenue vessel of its ordinary duties. . . . It is difficult to conceive that
discrimination could be made by the law between
services subjected to equally hazardous and équally
important military duties, both in time of peace and
in time of war. . . . Objection to granting pen-
sions for the revenue-marine officers and seamen
has been made, on the ground that such action
would be extending this bounty to civil employés of
the Government, a policy to which our legislative
traditions, so to speak, are opposed.   But, if in legal
theory they are civil employés, are they so in fact ?
Are they less positively a part of our military force in
time of war than the Army or Navy ?   It is true, revenue vessels are not to be ordered into action on purely
military service, offensive or defensive, except the
President so direct ; neither are vessels of the Navy.'

" The above clear and precise statement, showing
that the so-called Revenue Marine is simply a coast
navy, is without doubt correct and just, notwithstanding that the same subordinate in the Treasury
Department who formulated it for official communication to Congress, now makes the following assertion, though not, as it appears, with the endorse-
ment of the Secretary :

" 'The fact is, the business of the Revenue-Marine
officer is as distinct from that of a naval officer as
one land service is from another.   The military drill
and instruction of the Revenue-Marine officer do
not necessarily make him a naval officer any more
than the present education of a naval officer fits him
to manage vessels in harbors and along the shoal
waters of the coast.'

"Whether the views put forth in 1881, or the exactly opposite views emanating from the same person in 1883, are correct, and whether the service is to be considered as military or not, it is still unquestionably nautical; and it is for this reason that it comes within the scope of the general principle now advocated. It is because it forms a part of Government work in which officers and seamen are employed to navigate Government vessels, at sea, from port to port, that it may fitly become a part of the naval establishment. If the present system of military instruction is so defective that the officers of the revenue navy are not made naval officers, it would seem that some other system should be adopted to that end, seeing that they are "subjected to equally important and equally hazardous military duties, both in time of peace and in time of war," and that they are no less positively "a part of our military force in time of war than the Army or Navy." If, on the other hand, naval officers now have too little practice in coast navigation, a method should be devised of giving them such practice at once, for there is nothing more essential than this to success in the operations of modern warfare.

"The plan proposed with these objects in view included the transfer to the Navy Department of the cruising cutters, their officers and seamen (excepting the harbor boats used by the inspectors of customs, which do not require a special corps of officers); the organization of the officers transferred, as a Revenue-Marine Corps in the Navy, upon a footing precisely similar to that of the present naval officers; and the gradual employment of junior offi-

cers of the Navy in this service, as vacancies occur
at the bottom of the list. Such a measure would accomplish the desired result while protecting effectually the interests of the existing corps.

"The Life-Saving Service, being closely connected
with the Revenue Marine, and being equally work
of a nautical character, would necessarily follow the
latter. The objection which has been suggested
that naval officers are not surfmen, applies with
equal force to officers of the Revenue Marine. It is
obvious that one branch may be utilized in this service as readily as the other. The objection that a
necessary incompatibility exists between naval officers as such, and professional surfmen, which is not
to be found in the relations to the latter of Revenue-
Marine officers, requires no answer. The transfer of
the service involves no displacement of the crews of
life-saving stations; nor can any reason be adduced
why they should not perform as good work in saving
life endangered by the sea, under a department
charged with nautical matters, as under one whose
appropriate functions are the collection and dis-
bursement of the revenue, the issue of the currency,
and the regulation of the national debt.

"In view of the close and essential connection between the Navy and the Mercantile Marine, it was
further proposed to establish a Bureau of Mercantile
Marine in the Navy Department, which should be
charged with those branches of administration requiring a professional knowledge of the men and
materials employed in commercial navigation. Such
a bureau would include the registry, enrollment,
and license of vessels, their admeasurement for ton-

nage, the inspection of steam vessels, and the shipment and care of seamen. It should further be made the business of the proposed bureau, aided by a board representing the principal maritime and commercial interests, to exercise such care and supervision over these interests as would tend to a recovery of our carrying trade, and in general to the prosperity of our rapidly decaying merchant marine. The time has arrived when such a central administration is a necessity, as the merchant marine cannot prosper while its governmental regulation remains in the present chaotic condition. Whether its regulation should be intrusted to this or to another existing department, or to a new department created for it, is still an open question.

" The first plan was advocated upon three distinct grounds : first, that much of the work requires a special technical knowledge which it is the business of the Navy Department to have always at command ; secondly, that as the Navy is now charged with the protection and assistance of our shipping interests abroad, it might be wisely connected with the promotion of these interests at home ; and, finally, that as the merchant marine must always afford the sole reserve upon which, in emergencies, the Navy can draw to recruit its strength, the interests of the two are inseparably united.

" The recommendations made in the report of last year were followed by considerable discussion, of which a brief notice may fitly be taken. In some of the remonstrances presented by commercial and other organizations the various subjects were so confused and distorted, and the general purpose of

the recommendations was so entirely ignored that
the objections failed to have a bearing upon the
actual merits of the question.   Other remonstrances
were notoriously procured by persons who are
supported and given undue importance by the
existing system, and who were alarmed lest change
should destroy their occupations.[1]   In many instances the representations were not full or delib-
erate expressions of the opinion of the bodies whose
names were used.   Notably was this the case with
the resolutions of the Chamber of Commerce of
New York, where the mover of an adverse resolution became himself the chairman of the committee
to which the consideration of the measures was referred, and secured the adoption of a substantially
similar resolution by a vote of only 17 out of 740
members of the Chamber.

" Few of the arguments adduced by interested parties seem to have force against the broad general
proposition that the direction of these nautical subjects should be united, and that the nautical department of the Government should carry on the work.
The greater portion of them were based upon harsh
criticisms of the past management of the Navy Department, and of the conduct of officers and seamen
of the Navy.   To these no rejoinder will be here
engaged in, for an obvious reason.   The question
whether, as a permanent assignment, any particular

---

[1] This was especially seen in New York, where the author, in
arguments before a commercial committee, was met by misstate-
ments and misrepresentations claimed to have been supplied by
persons connected with the Revenue Marine and the Steam-Boat
Inspection Service.

subject-matter most appropriately belongs to one department or to another, must be settled on its merits,
upon the assumption that both departments either
are or will be ably and honestly conducted. Integrity and capacity in executive business are not
the exclusive possession of any one branch of the
Government, or of any one body of officials. To
say that naval officers cannot wisely be employed on
board the cruising cutters, whose principal use has
no relation to the appropriate business of the Treasury Department, because occasionally dutiable articles have been brought home in naval vessels, is
as unreasonable as to argue that the supervising inspectors should not inspect steam vessels, because,
in spite of their honesty and ability, terrible explo-
sions of boilers have taken place directly after their
most rigid examinations and unqualified certificates
of approval. The real point in the present question,
from which Congress should not be diverted by interested clamor, is : Ought these kindred branches
of the public service to be united ; and under which
of the two departments, when both are well-man-
aged, should they be most naturally and appropriately conducted ?

"To stigmatize naval officers as idlers who are
seeking to obtain an undue share of the civil administration is as unjust as it is illogical. If naval
officers are idlers, it is because idleness is enforced
upon them by a system which excludes them from
the occupations for which they are peculiarly fitted.
The remedy lies in giving them the employment
which the naval service proper, in time of peace,
cannot from its very nature fully afford. If they

desire to obtain such employment, the desire is
worthy and commendable. In the present case, the
charge against them of encroachment is without
foundation ; since the recommendations in this report have been made, not at the instance or solici-
tation of officers of the Navy, but, upon a careful
consideration, by the head of the Department, of
the principles that should govern their employment.

"If the Navy Department has not been wisely,
economically, and energetically administered, and if
naval officers have their faults or their vices, thorough reforms should be instituted, and such have
been and will be unsparingly recommended and
carried out. If they cannot be effected under the
present distribution of executive powers, and if, on
the other hand, the management of nautical affairs
is an appropriate attribute of fiscal administration,
then the existence of a separate nautical department
is an error which should be rectified by placing the
Navy under a bureau in the already comprehensive
Department of the Treasury. But whether attached
to one or to the other, all branches of nautical
administration should be united. As well might the
various parts of financial work be scattered among
different departments as the fragments of nautical
work be separated into an ocean navy here and a
coast navy there ; a survey of foreign coasts under
one department and a survey of our own under
another ; a bureau and an engineer corps for the
engines of naval steamers, and another bureau and
another engineer corps for those of merchant
steamers. Wherever the direction of nautical affairs

is placed, all its branches should be under a common head, and should work with a common purpose.

"One general argument has been presented against the transfer, in the form of an objection to employing military officers in civil duties. This is wholly out of place when applied to the army or navy of a popular government in a law-abiding community. In a despotism, where a standing army is maintained without the consent of the people and may be used for the repression of liberty, it would be wise to resist the extension of military employment to civil labors, even though the saving of expense should partly balance the evils resulting from an increase of despotic control. But in the United States the Army and Navy are the creation of the popular will. They are organized and supported only because the people deem them necessary for national existence and safety, and they can be disbanded at the pleasure of the people. They are equally with all other officials under the direction of a civil administration. They can therefore be wisely and safely employed in any work that will not impair their efficiency or discipline, and where their employment would save money that would otherwise be paid to maintain an unnecessary civil establishment. They should by all means be so employed when the service will not only relieve and benefit the people, but will add to the professional experience, and to the fitness for war duties, of the officers and men. Their exclusion can only be justified on the theory that to render them harmless they must be rendered inefficient ; a theory which, if carried out, would result in the immediate abolition of the service.

12

"The argument in favor of the full use of the Navy in all appropriate labors of peace becomes stronger as the nation seems more unlikely to engage in actual warfare. Our international policy tends to peace with all the world; our conflicts will be infrequent; and therefore more than all other nations we should utilize our officers, seamen, and ships in the nautical works which peace times require. Such are their appropriate sphere, not for their private benefit, but for the greater good of the Government to which they desire to give the fullest possible service.

"In presenting its recommendations last year, the Department made every effort to mature its opinion by the fullest and most exhaustive examination of the subject. Had it done otherwise it would have fallen short of its duty. The question has a vital bearing upon the improvement of the Navy, and is in no way dependent upon the character of administration for the time being in this or that department. It is a broad question of permanent policy and statesmanship. In such a spirit it has been dealt with here. It is not, perhaps, to be expected that such an extensive change will commend itself, at the first inspection, to the community and to Congress while those who live upon the existing system are seeking, by denunciatory methods, to create an unfavorable public sentiment. But it is believed that the advantages of the change, when impartially examined, will be recognized, and that it must ultimately be made. In such a confident belief the Department renews its recommendations, basing them not upon an appeal to popular prejudice, or upon recriminations, as odious as they are irrelevant, respecting the conduct of other branches of the public service, but upon a calm and candid consideration of the whole question, in the interests of a sound administrative policy, and of the efficiency of the naval arm of the Government as closely connected therewith."

Early in the present session of Congress Mr. Dingley of Maine introduced in the House of Representatives four important bills relating to shipping. The first is substantially the same as that passed by the last House—and which will be found among the appendices to this volume. It requires only the master of an American vessel to be a citizen and allows a minority ownership of an American vessel by aliens. It takes away from consuls the right to exact three months' extra wages on the discharge of a seaman, and provides instead that only the wages due shall be paid, except when a vessel is sold in a foreign port or a sailor is discharged by reason of ill-treatment by the officers of a vessel, in which cases one month's extra wages is to be paid. The right to ship a seaman for any port and discharge him at the expiration of the shipping agreement is recognized. The bill increases the compensation of vessels for transporting shipwrecked seamen in certain cases and abolishes consular fees for services to vessels and seamen, providing that consuls shall be paid from the Treasury. The mode of levying the tonnage tax is changed, this section being as follows :

"In lieu of all duties on tonnage, including light money, now imposed by law, a duty of three cents per ton, not to exceed in the aggregate fifteen cents

per ton in any one year, is hereby imposed at each
entry on all vessels which shall be entered in any
port of the United States from the West India Islands
or from any port or place in the Republic of Mexico,
or from any place south of Mexico down to and including Aspinwall and Panama, or from any port or
place in the dominion of Canada, or from the Sand-
wich Islands, and a duty of six cents per ton, not to
exceed in the aggregate thirty cents per ton in any
one year, is hereby imposed at each entry on all
vessels which shall be entered in the United States
from any other foreign port ; provided, that nothing
in this section shall be construed to repeal sections
2793 and 4220 of the Revised Statutes."

The bill reduces the Marine Hospital tax upon seamen engaged in the foreign carrying trade to twenty
cents per month instead of forty ; limits the individual liability of a ship-owner to the proportion of
all debts that his individual share of the vessel bears
to the whole, and the aggregate liabilities of all the
owners to the value of the vessel. It further provides that any fine, penalty, forfeiture, or exaction
upon a vessel when paid under protest may be recovered from the Treasury, on application within
one year, if the Secretary of the Treasury finds it
was illegally exacted. It also gives sailing vessels
the same privileges in unloading cargo that are extended to steamers. The last section of the bill exempts any sailing vessel under tow of a steam vessel
in charge of a licensed United States pilot from the
obligation to take or pay for the services of any pilot
under State laws.

The second bill authorizes the United States In-

spectors mentioned in Section 4442 of the Revised
Statutes, to examine and license masters of vessels
and others as pilots for sailing vessels in the coastwise trade upon the same terms and conditions, so
far as applicable, as pilots are now licensed for steam
vessels, and exempts vessels piloted by such licensed
pilots from taking or paying for the services of any
State pilot.

The third bill, "To encourage American ship-
building for the foreign carrying trade," extends the
act of 1872, admitting free of duty materials of
foreign production for the construction of wooden
vessels for the foreign carrying trade, so as to admit
in like manner all materials of foreign production
for the construction, equipment, repairs, and supplies
of iron and steel, as well as wooden vessels, for the
foreign trade. It also admits free of duty materials
of foreign production for the manufacture of articles
to be used in the construction and equipment of such
vessels, and also materials for the construction of
machinery for ship-yards and shops connected therewith.

The fourth bill establishes a Bureau of Commerce
and Navigation in the Treasury Department, and
authorizes the appointment by the President of a
Commissioner and Deputy Commissioner of Commerce and Navigation, with such clerks as the Secretary of the Treasury may detail from his present
force. The Commissioner of Commerce and Navigation, under the direction of the Secretary of the
Treasury, shall have general superintendence of
the commercial marine and merchant seamen of the
United States ; shall have charge of all questions

relating to the issue of registers, enrollments, and licenses of vessels ; shall have the supervision of the laws relating to the admeasurement of vessels, the assigning of letters and numbers thereto, and the interpretation and the execution of the laws relating to these subjects and to the tonnage tax. The Commissioner is also charged with so much of the duties heretofore imposed upon the Bureau of Statistics as relates to navigation and foreign commerce. He is also authorized to accept international rules for the commercial marine of the United States and to keep supervision of the navigable waters of the United States and report all obstructions. He is to prepare annually and publish a list of vessels of the United States, and is authorized to change the names of vessels. The Commissioner of Commerce and Navigation is required to investigate the working of the laws relating to navigation and to report such particulars in their operation as may, in his judgment, admit of improvement or require amendment. If this initial step in establishing a Bureau of Commerce and Navigation should be approved by Congress, Mr. Dingley hopes that in due time all other boards and officials charged with duties relating to the merchant marine of the United States will be brought within the control of this bureau, so that the Government may have a department similar to the British Board of Trade, charged with the duty of guarding the interests of shipping.

The provisions of these bills are excellent in some particulars, and are undoubtedly tendencies in a right direction ; in details, however, and in want of breadth they are open to criticism, the justice of

which will stand or fall by the arguments already
advanced. The Secretary of the Navy must undoubtedly be gratified that his statesmanlike principles of administration are bearing such good fruit,
for surely in a future, not distant, right-thinking
men everywhere will accept the plan proposed by
him as the true one. The special objections to the
Bill which seeks to establish a Bureau of Commerce
and Navigation in the Treasury Department are
based upon the facts that the practical control is
given to officials whose lack of special training renders their fitness questionable ; that a specific branch
of government is made a part of a Department
which already administers enormous and most
varied interests ; and that a new bureau is created
while an old one exists, which is co-central in its
purposes and is already possessed of such special
advantages for the work that its control of the merchant marine will not involve its own affairs with
those of any other department.

And with the restoration of the Merchant Marine
the elevation of the Navy should go hand in hand.
The people of this country are most willing, nay most
anxious, to recreate their Navy and no Congressional
action would be more popular ; but the fear of a
Democratic House of Representatives that its appropriations on the eve of a national election will be
handled by a Republican Executive, through his
Secretaries, seems to be so important that every other
consideration is consigned to a limbo of political
expediency. But can we hesitate longer? The
present condition of our fleet makes it necessary
that the work of reconstruction should go on as

rapidly as possible On foreign stations we have less than twenty cruising vessels, and with nothing at home to replace them.   Therefore, besides the three vessels now building, seven additional unarmored steel cruisers should be begun, three of which should conform to the types illustrated by the Chicago, Boston, and Dolphin, and four should be heavily armed cruising gunboats of about 1,500 tons displacement, with good speed.

The nucleus of the armored fleet now represented by the doubled turretted Monitors Puritan, Amphitrite, Terror, Monadnock, and Miantonomah should be increased by the construction of three steel rams, three cruising and six harbor torpedo boats; and the standard fixed by the first Advisory Board in 1881, viz.: a fleet of forty-three cruising ships, with a reserve of twenty-seven, should be adopted. To reach this total of seventy war ships would require the building of forty-five vessels, and in order to keep abreast with the march of improvement at least seven of these should be constructed yearly for the next ten years.   Under this plan the country would find itself in 1894, by a yearly expenditure of $4,283,000 and with an annual construction of 13,500 tons, in the possession of a modern steel navy, "in every way adequate to the maintenance of the safety and honor of the nation."

Then with a legitimate commerce protected and aided by a competent naval force we can assume our old place among the nations of the world. Insolent and jealous rivals and snarling enemies can be taught the lessons so long needed ; and when the next century dawns upon a nation of seventy millions of freemen who illustrate the wisdom and confirm the prophecy of our forefathers, this country will have the power to assert the natural rights of man wherever such may be assailed. Prosperity on land is the handmaiden of power át sea, and whose is the ocean, his also are the lands around and about it. Action, action, action is needed, but vain is the call, as of old, unless the people command the change ; for Congress will consider only the political bearings of the great question, and will never consent to the restoration of the merchant marine and to the golden wedding of the two services until the citizens of this Government, which is of the people, for the people, and by the people, demand in trumpet tones, "FREE SHIPS AND SAILORS' RIGHTS."

APPENDIX I.

In the Congress of 1881, upon motion of Mr. Perry Belmont, a committee was appointed to inquire into the condition and wants of American ship-building and ship-owning interests, and to investigate the causes of the decline of the American foreign carrying trade. Contrary to usual custom, Mr. Belmont was not made a member of the Joint Committee appointed by both Houses—a reversal of precedent that excited much invidious comment. After various meetings the Committee, on December 15, 1882, submitted the following report :—

Your committee assembled in New York City August 11th, and, for the purpose of furthering the investigation which they were directed to make in the recess, extended a public invitation to all persons possessing information on the subjects of inquiry to furnish the committee with written replies to the following interrogatories :—

First.—Why cannot this country build iron, steel, or wooden vessels as well and as cheaply as they are built in Scotland, England, or other countries?

Second.—If we have such vessels, without cost to us, can they be run by us in competition with those of other countries who build their own vessels and run them with their own officers and crews, without a modification or repeal of existing laws?

Third.—What modifications of existing laws or what new laws are required to remove discriminations against and burdens upon our shipping and ship-owning interests, such as customs dues, port dues, consular charges, pilotage, tonnage, and other dues, etc.?

Fourth.—Compare the laws of other countries with our own with a view to their effect upon our and their shipping and ship-owning interests ?

Fifth.—Should our navigation laws be repealed or modified, and if modified, wherein and for what purpose ?

Sixth.—What is the cost of the component materials of iron, steel, or wooden vessels in other countries and our own?

Seventh.—What would be the effect of a rebate on any or all such material ?

Eighth.—Present any other statements connected with the cause of the decline of the American foreign carrying trade, and what remedies can be applied by legislation ?

After taking measures to give a wide publicity to this invitation through the press and to forward the interrogatories to a large number of persons, in various parts of the Union, supposed to be practically acquainted with the subject, the committee adjourned to reassemble in New York City November 15th, and during their six days' session in that city the efforts to obtain all possible information were cordially seconded by representatives of the associations interested in American shipping, and by gentlemen interested in the prosperity of the ship-building and ship-owning industries of the United States.

The exhaustive and very valuable statements and statistics accompanying this report bear witness not only to the cordiality with which the inquiry has been welcomed, but also to the deep interest felt by the American people in the adoption of measures calculated to improve the condition of our foreign carrying trade. The official tables appended to this report furnish an accurate statement of the condition of the American merchant marine engaged in the foreign and coastwise trade and in the fisheries for each fiscal year from 1840 to and including 1882, so far as the same is shown by the tonnage employed in each, the value of the exports and imports which make up our foreign commerce, and the share of these carried in American vessels.

The following figures for each semi-decennial year since

1840 will present at a glance the facts relating to the past and present condition of American shipping :

Year.	Tonnage in Foreign Trade.	Tonnage in Coastwise Trade.	Value of Exports and Imports.	Per Cent. carried in American Vessels.	Per Cent. carried in Foreign Vessels.
1840..	762,838	1,172,694	$231,227,465	82.9	17.1
1845..	904,476	1,223,218	231,901,170	81.7	18.3
1850..	1,439,694	1,797,825	330,037,038	72.5	17.5
1855..	2,348,358	2,543,255	536,625,366	75.6	14.4
1860..	2,378,396	2,644.867	762,288,550	66.5	33.5
1865..	1,518,350	3,318,522	604,412,996	27.7	62.3
1870..	1,448,846	2,638,247	991,896,889	35.6	64.4
1875..	1,515,998	2,219,698	1,219,434,544	25.8	74.2
1880..	1,314,402	2,637,686	1,613,770,633	17.4	82.6
1881..	1,297,035	2,646.011	1,675.024.318	16.0	84.0
1882..	1,259,492	2,873,638	1,567,071,700	15.5	84.5

THE COASTWISE MARINE.

The above table indicates nearly as prosperous a condition of our merchant marine engaged in the coastwise trade, to which only American vessels are admitted, as is found in other domestic industries. The amount of trade, to be sure, is but little larger now than before the war ; but as a much larger proportion of it is now composed of steamers than was the case twenty-five years ago, the carrying capacity is increased very much more than the comparison of tonnage would indicate. The rapid extension of our railroad system within a quarter of a century has also diverted to land conveyance a large proportion of the freight formerly carried by sailing vessels. When it is borne in mind that during the past decade the number of freight cars employed on railroads in the United States has increased 120 per cent., so that to-day their freight capacity is nearly three times that of the vessels employed in our coastwise, including the lake and river trade, the slow growth of the latter interest is fully accounted for. Some burdens have, however, been pointed out to your committee, which ought to

be removed from our coastwise marine to enable it to
compete on equal conditions with common carriers on the
· land.

THE FOREIGN TRADE.

The foregoing official table presents a very unsatisfactory
and humiliating condition of the American merchant marine
employed in the foreign carrying trade. While our foreign
commerce has steadily increased—the value of our exports
and imports the last fiscal year having been seven times as
much as it was in 1855, and more than twice as much as it
was in 1860—yet the share of these exports and imports
carried in American vessels has decreased from 82.9 per
cent. in 1840 to 15.5 per cent. in 1882. Of this loss 16.4
per cent. was before the breaking out of the civil war in
1861 ; 38.8 per cent. during the four years of the war, and
12.2 per cent. since the close of the war. The decline experienced between 1845 and 1850 was largely recovered between 1850 and 1855 ; but from 1856 the decline was continuous, although slow up to 1861, when it became so rapid
and serious, in consequence of the civil war and the operations of the Confederate cruisers, that between 1861 and
1865 we lost more than one-third of our foreign carrying
trade. Between 1865 and 1870 there was some improvement, mainly brought about by a return of vessels to the
foreign trade, which had been employed during the war in
Government service and the coastwise trade. Between 1870
and 1875 the share of the foreign carrying trade controlled
by American vessels declined 9.8 per cent.; between 1875
and 1880 the decline was 8.4 per cent., and in the past two
years it has been 1.9 per cent.

The growth of American tonnage engaged in the foreign
carrying trade practically ceased in 1855. Before that period
it had increased for many years at the rate of about twelve
per cent. per annum, but between 1855 and 1860, notwithstanding our exports and imports increased eight per cent.
per annum or forty per cent. during the five years, our ton-

nage employed in the foreign carrying trade remained almost stationary, and the ship-building industry, so far as it was directed to the construction of vessels for the foreign trade, rapidly declined. In 1855 our tonnage employed in the foreign trade was 2,348,358 tons, and in 1860 it was only 2,379,396, thus barely holding its own. In 1855 there were 507 vessels of the classes usually employed in the foreign trade built in the United States; in 1856 the number declined to 463; in 1857 it declined to 309; in 1858 to 168, and in 1859 to 117.

During the four years of civil war the American tonnage employed in the foreign trade declined from 2,496,894 tons in 1861 to 1,518,350 tons in 1865, a loss of 978,544 tons, or nearly forty per cent. The decline of this tonnage since 1865 has been about 15.5 per cent., notwithstanding the value of our foreign commerce has increased from $604,412,996 in 1865 to $1,567,022,700 in 1882.

CAUSES OF THE DECLINE.

The decline of our foreign carrying trade dates from 1855, although the causes which produced it gathered volume so slowly as to attract little attention for several years. What these causes were appears from an investigation of the maritime history of the commercial world, and particularly of England, between 1840 and 1860. Up to 1850–55 the ocean trade was carried on exclusively in wooden sailing vessels. To be sure, a few ocean iron steamships had been constructed between 1836 and 1845, but the prejudice against them was so strong that it was not till between 1845 and 1855 that they began to gain a secure position on the ocean. The success of iron steamships gave to England an opportunity to seize upon the carrying trade of the world, which she was not slow to take advantage of. So long as wooden sailing vessels engrossed the ocean trade the United States had the advantage in possessing cheaper materials for ship-building over every other maritime nation. But when it was

discovered that iron could take the place of wood, and steam
could be successfully substituted for sails in ocean freighting,
then the tables were turned, because of the fact that England
possessed such extensive iron and coal mines near the sea,
with cheap labor to work them. These advantages, however, would not have availed England in the start if her
Government had not come to the aid of her shipping interests by liberal mail pay, and even by guaranteeing seven
and eight per cent. dividends to capitalists; and thus the
English Government secured the establishment of steamship lines to all parts of the world. Parliament in 1854 established a Board of Trade, with its president a member of
the Ministry, for the sole purpose of looking after the interests of British commerce and British shipping. The merchant shipping laws of the United Kingdom were revised so
as to remove every burden from her merchant marine, and
afford every possible facility for gaining possession of the
ocean.

It is not surprising that the great advantage given England by the change in the ocean carrying trade from wood
to iron and sail to steam, so signally strengthened by the
co-operation and material aid of the British Government, and
met only by a policy of inaction on the part of the Government of the United States, should have begun to check the
growth of our tonnage for several years prior to 1860.

It is probable, however, that if the civil war had not come
upon us just as we began to realize that our foreign carrying
trade had ceased to grow, while that of England was rapidly
extending, some measures would have been taken to regain
the advantages which we were beginning to lose. But at this
crisis the civil war came upon us, and not only engrossed
our energies and capital from 1861 to 1865, but also swept
from the ocean more than one-third of all the deep-sea tonnage which we possessed at the opening of the struggle.
Great as was the loss to our merchant marine by the direct
influence of the war, yet more serious still was the injury it
inflicted on us by the opportunity that it gave England to

build up great iron ship-yards and gain possession of the channels of trade at a time when our hands were tied. Even after the war closed a depreciated currency, inflated prices, and the high taxation necessary to pay the expenses of the conflict of arms, made it difficult to devise any policy to revive our shipping interests. To add to our difficulties the extraordinary profit afforded capital and labor by the opening up of the far West made the more moderate profits of the foreign carrying trade undesirable for investors. It was not till our currency had settled down to a specie basis and restored normal prices, and not till the far West ceased to offer so exceptional opportunities for investment, and the rate of interest dropped to the point where it has remained for a few years past, that any legislative measures could be devised which would be likely to attract capital to the foreign carrying trade.

DIFFICULTIES TO BE OVERCOME.

In considering what remedies for the prostrate condition of our foreign carrying trade are within the reach of legislation, it is obvious that the difficulty of the problem is greatly increased by the fact that England has had more than a quarter of a century the start of us in working out her comprehensive and ingenious policy of building up her merchant marine employed in the foreign trade since iron and steam began to revolutionize the transportation. However wise may be any plan of relief and encouragement, it is obvious that the revival must be slow. But the stake is so great in its economical aspects and so vital to our national growth and safety, that no effort should be spared to accomplish the end which Congress had in view when this investigation was ordered.

The foreign carrying trade, unlike the protected coastwise trade and all other domestic industries, is on the great highway of the ocean, where competition is open to the whole world. The nation which can carry on this trade the

most efficiently and at the least cost to shippers will control
it, and in controlling it will command the ocean. By our
ability to build vessels as cheap as other nations so long as
wood was the material of which they were constructed, and
by our ability to sail them as economically as others so long
as sailing vessels engrossed the ocean trade, and the British
Government left her merchant marine to take care of itself,
as our Government always has, the United States had a
proud position on the ocean. We lost that position when
these conditions passed away. If we are to revive our foreign carrying trade and assume the place on the ocean to
which we are entitled, we must make it feasible to build the
kind of vessels required for the foreign trade so that they
will cost our ship-owners no more than they cost to foreign
owners.

CONSTRUCTION OF VESSELS.

If wooden sailing vessels controlled the ocean trade as
they did twenty-five years ago, there would be no problem
of the construction of vessels to solve. We can build to-day
first-class wooden sailing vessels as cheaply as they can be
built elsewhere, as we did before the war ; but notwithstanding such vessels will always be used extensively in the coastwise trade, and to a restricted extent in the foreign trade,
yet it is obvious that iron steamships are to largely control
the ocean carrying trade of the world. Year by year, as improvements have been made to economize fuel, steamships
have improved more and more, until to-day they command
the trade of the North Atlantic. All of the practical gentlemen who appeared before your committee agreed that it
now costs on the average $10 to $15 per ton more to build
an iron sailing vessel and from $25 to $35 per ton more to
build an iron steamship in the United States than it costs
on the Clyde. They all agreed that the chief cause of this
excess of cost is due to the fact that the labor required to
mine, smelt and make the iron and fashion it into the form
of the steamship costs considerably more in the United

States than it does on the Clyde. If we had been called upon to build iron steamships before the war we should have found the same difficulty in competing with Great Britain in a manufacture requiring so large an amount of labor as does the building of iron steamers from the ore and coal in the bed. Among other causes named was the fact that the small demand for iron vessels—for the reason that England's experience, start, and other advantages enable her to build and sail vessels more cheaply than we can—gives little encouragement to investment of the large amount of capital needed to establish and extend iron ship-yards, stimulate the inventive genius of our people, and overcome the obstacles always encountered in inaugurating new industries.

It is conceded by all that no remedy can be effective or wise which does not look to the development of shipbuilding in the United States and to making it practicable to build iron vessels in this country for the foreign trade at a cost to the owners no greater than that of similar ships of our rivals. Every remedy suggested is urged largely on the ground that it will ultimately accomplish this result. Nothing is better settled than the fact that no nation can gain or long hold a strong position on the ocean unless it builds its own ships. Any nation which relies on another nation for its supply of ships loses in time of peace its commercial independence, and in time of war places its very existence at the mercy of the powers which command the ocean. In endeavoring to devise a policy which will build up the iron ship-building industry in the United States, and supply our ship-owners with such vessels as they may want for the foreign trade at a cost no greater than the cost of vessels run by their competitors, your committee have found more or less difference of opinion among ourselves as to what would be the wisest and most efficient plan. Feeling the grave importance of an earnest effort to provide a remedy for the decadence of the American carrying trade, and recognizing that there must be some yielding of personal views if anything is to be done, your committee, without waiving the individual right of any member to favor additional remedies, have united in recommending the adoption by Congress of the plan as laid down in section 18 of the bill presented, providing for the payment of a drawback on American material used equal to the duty if it had been foreign material.

For the purpose of illustrating what would be the practical working of the foregoing plan, we have obtained from the Delaware River Iron Ship Building and Engine Works a schedule of the materials actually used in constructing two first-class passenger and freight steamships for the Pacific trade of 2,131 tons each, having a speed of thirteen knots. It appears that 3,709,845 pounds of iron, mainly in the form of plates, angles, and bars, were used in the construction of the hull, engines, boilers, etc., of each steamship. The duty on iron, if imported in these forms, would average under the present tariff about $26 for each ton of the steamship. The duty on the other materials used in the hull, equipment and furniture, would carry the drawback allowed from the Treasury to about $34. As the cost of each of the steamships to which we have referred was $286,317, or $134 per ton, the net cost under the foregoing plan, after deducting the drawback, would be about $100 per ton, which, from all the information obtained by your committee, would be substantially the cost of a similar steamship built upon the Clyde. If the steamship were intended only for freighting, with the speed of seven or eight knots, as usually found in English freighting steamers, the quantity of iron used, the drawback, and the cost would be considerably reduced. In the case of iron sailing vessels the drawback would be about $15 per ton. That the proposed drawback, therefore, will practically affect the increased cost of building an iron steamship in the United States over its cost on the Clyde is the unanimous judgment of ship-builders and owners of the Board of Trade of San Francisco (which proposed this plan), the Maritime Association of New York, and other commercial boards.

So far as the original cost of any kind of a vessel affects the question of the restoration of the American flag to its proper position on the ocean, there is good reason to believe that the policy proposed will solve the problem. It should be borne in mind, however, that the United States Treasury receives annually about $1,500,000 from the tax on tonnage engaged in the foreign trade. This tax is not imposed on vessels engaged in the coastwise trade or on any other industry. In 1880 the tonnage tax yielded $1,490,544, of which $237,863 was paid by American vessels. During the last fiscal year the amount of the tax was little less, but it is certain to increase as our foreign commerce enlarges. There would be a general concurrence in the justice of abolishing the tax were it not for the fact that England and most foreign nations impose a similar tonnage tax on all vessels entering their ports, and the further fact that five-sixths of our tonnage tax is paid by foreign and only one-sixth by American vessels ; and on account of reciprocal commercial treaties the tax cannot be abolished on our own vessels without also working abolition as to foreign vessels. We can, however, and should use the tax or its equivalent to encourage our own merchant marine employed in the foreign trade. This was precisely what England did when she granted $10,000,000 out of her tonnage tax to make the Clyde the most favorable location in the world for iron ship-building.

On the reasonable supposition that the tonnage tax will amount to $10,000,000 during the next five years, this alone would meet the drawback demands under the plan proposed for at least 400,000 tons of new steamships and sailing vessels for the foreign trade during that period. This increase of tonnage would itself go far to revive our foreign carrying trade without taking a single dollar from the ordinary revenue. If the addition to our tonnage should be more than this the additional appropriations required would be wisely expended. From any point of view the experiment is one which affords much promise and, in view of the general indorsement which it has received from boards of trade and commercial men and the national importance of the end sought to be reached, ought to be given a thorough trial. If, in addition to this direct aid, the United States shall imitate Great Britain in giving contracts to private ship-yards to build a portion of any steel war ship which it may be deemed wise to construct for our navy, there is reason and hope that favorable results would follow. As it is essential for our iron and steel ship-yards to place themselves in a position to secure contracts for building vessels for South America, and perhaps other foreign countries, your committee recommend that a drawback of ninety per cent. be allowed on any imported materials of a vessel constructed in the United States for foreign account. The law as it now stands (section 3019, Revised Statutes) allows such a drawback in the case of a vessel or other article wholly constructed of imported material. As many of the materials of such a vessel can be obtained at home as cheaply as abroad, and would be preferred by the builder of a vessel for foreign account, it is wise to allow a drawback, so far as imported materials are concerned, when the vessel is built partly of foreign and partly of domestic material.

The other problem which must be satisfactorily solved relates to the successful running of American vessels in the foreign trade after they are built. After a policy has been inaugurated which will secure to America sail and steam vessels at no higher cost than those owned by our rivals, such a consummation will not revive the carrying trade of the United States unless we can maintain and sail these vessels under our law at no higher cost to the owner than English ship-owners can sail their vessels under British laws. That we have not been able to do this for many years is evident from the fact that, notwithstanding we have built first-class modern sailing vessels for nearly ten years as cheaply as our foreign competitors, yet we have been gradually driven from the ocean by foreign sailing vessels as well as by foreign steamships. More than half of our exports and imports are still carried by sailing vessels, and yet American vessels

carry but little more than a third of this half. To be sure, it is
only in this branch of carrying trade that we make any showing, but the slow and steady decline of even our sailing tonnage employed in the foreign trade and the unanimous voice
of our ship-owners bear witness to the disadvantages under
which we have labored. The evidence presented to your
committee shows that a large part of the obstacles to the successful recovery of American vessels in competition with
English ships may be overcome by modifying our shipping
laws, removing burdens, and giving the same privileges as
to ships' supplies and the same compensation as to mail service as the English laws have given for a quarter of a century. Up to 1854 the English laws relating to shipping were
substantially the same as ours. At that time the English
Parliament began a complete revision of her merchant shipping statutes, so as to remove every obstacle and give every
facility to British shipping, and from year to year, as the
Board of Trade has recommended, England has been legislating in the interest of her merchant marine. During this
whole period nothing has been done by the American Congress to meet England in this direction. Our merchant
shipping laws remain substantially the same as they were
originally framed more than four score years ago. They
were all that were needed so long as the English laws were the
same. Our error was in not imitating England, so as to give
our merchant marine the same advantages in this respect
that English shipping enjoys ; and our further error was that
when steamships began to take the place of sailing vessels
we did not also imitate England in extending the same encouragement for the establishment of American steamship
lines that she did for her own, although the adoption of such
a policy after England has intrenched herself in her position
on the ocean for a quarter of a century, your committee believe would gradually work most beneficial results. At least
it would remove all legislative obstructions to the revival of
our foreign carrying trade, and would leave American enterprise and capital free to enter into competition for a due

share of ocean transportation. Your committee, therefore, unanimously recommend a modification of our laws relating to the American merchant marine employed in the foreign trade in the following particulars :—

THREE MONTHS' EXTRA WAGES.

Under old laws enacted at a time when the sailors of our merchant marine were all American, and not, as now, ninety per cent. foreigners ; when shipping agreements were for the round voyage, and not as now, generally from port to port ; and when the means of communication abroad with the ports of the United States were infrequent and dilatory, an American vessel from which a seaman is discharged by a United States Consul is practically required to pay such seaman three months' extra wages, two-thirds of which go to the seaman and one-third to the Government. The facts brought to the attention of your committee by a large number of ship-owners, masters, and others made it clear that what was formerly a wise law, rarely appealed to by any sailor, has now, in the changed condition of our foreign trade, become a serious burden on American vessels and a positive injury to the morals of the crews. The burden consists not simply in the large amount of money exacted, but also, and more injuriously, in the annoying delays and contentions arising from hearings before consuls and consular officers. Your committee recommend that the law be so modified as to provide that the vessel shall pay one month's wages, or provide adequate employment on a returning vessel, or provide a passage home to a seaman discharged from an American vessel in a foreign port. When a seaman is injured in the line of duty or contracts disease in consequence of want of proper provision on shipboard, the vessel is only to be responsible for the payment of all the expenses of sickness and medical attendance. When a seaman is discharged by the United States Consul in the port which he expressly contracted should be the end of his service, there is no reason why the consular officer should exact extra wages from the vessel under any pretext. When a seaman is discharged by the Consul, on the application of the former, there seems no just ground for requiring the vessel to pay extra wages except the causes named in the bill proposed, and in no other case ought the Consul to have power to exact extra wages or charges from a vessel. To give every consular officer—many of them foreigners—authority to impose such a charge upon a vessel whenever a discharge is granted to a seaman " in accordance with the general principles or usages of maritime law," as arbitrarily construed by such official, without the right of appeal, as section 4580 of the Revised Statutes of the United States now does, is to put an improper power into the hands of men who may have an interest in the decision, and many of whom in the smaller and more remote ports are unfitted to exercise so broad a discretion. No other government imposes such a burden on its merchant marine, and the imposition of it on ours works in practice a serious discrimination against American vessels. In reporting amendments of our laws in this direction your committee have followed the English law, which does justice to the vessel and at the same time amply protects the seamen.

The law (section 4578, Revised Statutes) as it now stands compels every American vessel to convey wrecked, disabled, or destitute American sailors from a foreign port to the United States on request of a United States Consul, and allows not exceeding $10 for this service. This may be sufficient for the care, transportation, and rations of a disabled sailor on a voyage of a few days, but for a long voyage imposes a serious loss on the vessel. Your committee recommend an amendment of this law, authorizing the collector of the port in the United States where the seaman is landed to pay additional compensation, not to exceed fifty cents per day, in cases where the length of the voyage requires.

Your committee further recommend a prohibition of the payment of advance wages or giving advance notes on the shipment of seamen. As is well known, these advance wages almost uniformly go to the sailor's landlord, who is thus enabled to strip the seaman not only of the wages already earned and paid, but also of the wages which he is yet to earn ; worse still, it is the fund from which the blood-money system and other evils come that are a shame to civilization. A report made to the House of Representatives by the Committee of Commerce at the first session of the Forty-seventh Congress, presents the necessity of this legislation so clearly that we need not pursue the subject further. The law (section 4131, Revised Statutes) requires that not only the master or captain, but also all other officers of an American vessel, shall under all circumstances be citizens of the United States. This is wise as to the master, but it has been represented to your committee that cases frequently arise in which one of the mates dies or is disabled, when it is necessary to supply his place with an experienced foreign seaman. Your committee is of the opinion that no useful end is advanced by a requirement which fetters an American vessel in the foreign trade, and therefore recommends the modification of the laws so as to apply only to captains and masters. Under existing law the liability of a part owner of a vessel is that of a partner and therefore unlimited. The English law limits the liability of a part owner of a vessel to the proportion of any and all debts and liabilities that his individual share of the vessel bears to the whole, on the ground that as the business of a vessel must necessarily be committed to an agent removed from his principals, as in a corporation, it is just that the part owner should be required as a shareholder rather than as a partner. As it appears to your committee that our law bears too heavily on the part owner of a vessel and discourages investments in vessel property, your committee recommend the adoption of substantially the English principle of limited liability. The excellent marine hospital service in the United States is supported by a tax of forty cents per month on each seaman in both foreign and coastwise marine (section 4585, Revised Statutes), which is paid by the vessel and deducted from the seaman's wages. Before 1871 this tax was twenty cents per month. As the indirect effect of this tax is to give English vessels, which are not required to pay a hospital tax, an advantage in hiring seamen, if it does not increase the wages of seamen on American vessels, your committee recommend the reduction of the tax to the former limit of twenty cents.

Your committee recommend the abolition of the tonnage tax as to vessels engaged in trade with the Dominion of Canada. The law now practically exempts from this tax a large portion of the vessels engaged in this trade on the lakes, and inasmuch as the trade is in the nature of a coastwise trade and carried on in direct competition with railroads, justice seems to require that the exemption be made general so far as the trade with Canada is concerned.

Under the laws consular officers are paid from the fund derived from fees exacted from American ships and merchants in foreign ports. Indeed, in 1882, not only was our consular service, costing $889,840, paid from these fees, but also $51,018 surplus was left in the Treasury for application to other government expenses. About $100,000 of these fees came from American shipping. In the same period England appropriated over $1,000,000 from her Treasury for the support of her consular service, which is maintained in every port of the world mainly to extend British commerce and aid British shipping. The charges imposed by the British consular officers on English vessels are very small.

Your committee think it would be wise to abolish all fees for services to American vessels and sailors, even if this involves a slight charge on the Treasury for the maintenance of our consular system for the present and until a system of paying all consular officers by salaries can be arranged. If thought proper, such officers, when paid in whole or in part by fees, may be required to make a detailed report to the State Department of service performed to American vessels and sailors, with the fees heretofore allowed for such services, and be allowed from the Treasury the same amount which they would have received under the fee system.

Our laws authorize the importation in bond free of duty of all materials needed for the repair of vessels engaged in the foreign carrying trade, but they make no provision for a similar rebate of duty on ships' supplies of vessels engaged in such foreign trade as do the English laws. Your committee recommend an amendment of section 2514 so as cover ships' supplies as well as materials for repairs.

The law as it exists (section 3976, R. S.) compels the master of every American vessel engaged in the foreign trade to carry such United States mails as may be tendered him by the Post-office Department, and allows him as compensation for such service a sum not exceeding two cents per letter carried. In no case is this an adequate compensation and in some instances it does not pay the cost to the vessel of delivering the mails at the post-office in the port of arrival. The pay to United States vessels in the foreign trade for transporting the mails in 1880 was only 2¼ cents per mile, while at the same time the steamers on our coast which contracted to carry the mails received 57¼ cents per mile for the mail service. The contrast between our inadequate mail pay to American vessels engaged in the foreign trade and the very liberal mail pay given by Great Britain to her steamship lines only serves to show more clearly the injustice and unwisdom of our policy. Since 1840 England has paid more than $250,000,000 for mail service, with the deliberate purpose of establishing and maintaining steamship lines to connect the United Kingdom with all parts of the world. In one year she has paid about $3,000,000 to her steamship lines for mail service, which was $1,641,300 more than she received from mail matter transported by them.

As this subject is before the Postal Committee of both the Senate and the House, we refrain from reporting any legislation, but unanimously recommend such a modification of our laws as will give fair compensation to American vessels in the foreign trade which may carry our mails, and adequate pay for mail service to American steamship lines that are already or may be hereafter established.

TAXATION OF VESSELS BY STATE AUTHORITY.

There is no one thing that has had more to do in rendering it difficult to sail an American vessel in competition with an English steamship than the different system of taxation of shipping as well as other invested capital in the two countries. The English system of taxation is on incomes; ours on the value of the property. For example, a steamship valued at $500,000 and earning eight per cent. net, or $40,000 annually, would pay in England an income tax of about two per cent., or only $800. A similar steamship, under the laws of every State but Massachusetts and New York (which have recently exempted vessels from local taxation engaged in the foreign trade), and possibly Pennsylvania, would pay a tax of about two per cent. on the value, or $10,000. Thus in the single item of taxation the steamship under the English flag would have every year an advantage of $9,200, which in so close a business as the foreign carrying trade would of itself be enough to make it impossible to sail an American steamship in competition with an English rival.

Your committee are unanimously of the opinion that it is of vital importance to the revival of the American foreign carrying trade that this difficulty should be removed either by State or federal legislation.

Your committee think that the element of local taxation enters so largely into the solution of the problem of sailing American vessels, that it is incumbent on Congress to exercise the power of regulating commerce, which it possesses under the constitution, to the extent of prohibiting State and municipal taxation of vessels engaged in the foreign trade.

BUREAU OF COMMERCE AND NAVIGATION.

The English merchant marine and English commerce have been greatly aided by the watchful supervision and regulations of the British Board of Trade, whose president is a member of the Cabinet. In the executive department of our Government we have no board or bureau with similar duties and power, and none which is required by law to even keep a watchful eye over the interests of our shipping, except for purposes of collecting the revenues. Whether it would not be wise to establish in the Treasury Department a Bureau or Board of Commerce and Navigation, of which the Secretary of the Treasury should be the official head, with powers and duties in some respects akin to those of the British Board of Trade, is already under consideration by the Committees on Commerce of the Senate and House, and will undoubtedly receive the attention it deserves.

It is unnecessary for your committee to dwell on the great importance of any and all legislative measures that will tend to a revival of the American foreign carrying trade and a restoration of the American flag to a position on the ocean commensurate with our population, wealth, and rank in the family of nations.

The problem presented to Congress involves interests of exceptional importance ; the great agricultural interests of the West and South are especially concerned. To-day at least eighty-five per cent of their products exported to other countries depend on foreign vessels, mainly English, for transportation ; and unless something is speedily done to relieve American shipping engaged in the foreign trade, our dependence on English ocean steamers will be complete. This places our commerce at the mercy of England. In case of war between that country and another power able to put cruisers on the ocean, American farmers and American people as a whole would suffer nearly as much as the belligerents by having their exports and imports in British bottoms liable to capture and confiscation. In its material aspects the shipping problem is national and in no sense local.

It is more than a business question. It is one which affects our rank and influence as a nation. A nation is known and felt outside of its own boundaries more by the flag which floats at the masthead of its merchant marine than by anything else. It is difficult to conceive the loss which we suffer, not only in national prestige, but also in commercial importance, by the infrequency with which American vessels appear in foreign ports.

The problem concerns our national independence and safety. In modern times the seal of power of every nation is on the rocking waves as well as on the solid land. The naval power of every country will in the long run be proportionate to its merchant marine. In building up our foreign carrying trade, therefore, we strengthen the defences of the nation and give new security to our Republic.

While some of the members of your committee do not concur in all the statements and reasonings of the foregoing report, and would recommend additional legislation, yet all concur in recommending the passage of the accompanying bill.

O. D. CONGER, Chairman.
WARNER MILLER.
G. G. VEST.
H. J. PAGE.
GEORGE M. ROBESON.
NELSON DINGLEY, JR.
ROBERT M. McLANE.
S. S. COX.

APPENDIX II.

THE REVIVAL OF THE AMERICAN CARRYING TRADE.—
AN ANSWER TO THE QUESTIONS OF THE JOINT
COMMITTEE OF CONGRESS, APPOINTED TO INQUIRE
INTO THE CONDITION AND WANTS OF AMERICAN
SHIP-BUILDING AND SHIP-OWNING INTERESTS.

BY JOHN CODMAN.

MR. CHAIRMAN AND GENTLEMEN:

Although I have not seen the text of the joint resolution authorizing the appointment of your committee, it is gratifying to be able to infer from the circular I have the honor to receive from you, that you have been delegated to consider two separate and distinct questions which Congress has heretofore regarded as united. Ship-building is one industry, ship-owning is another. It is desirable that our country should have both; but if we cannot have the former, you will admit that it is folly to deprive ourselves of the latter.

Your first question is:

Why cannot this country build iron, steel, or wooden vessels as well and as cheaply as they are built in Scotland, England, or other countries?

ANSWER. We can and do build wooden vessels as well and as cheaply as vessels of a good quality are built elsewhere, and cheaper than they can be built in Great Britain. It was for this very reason, in days before the era of extensive iron ship-building, that England repealed her navigation laws, which were then similar to our own, in order that her people might still have their share of the carrying trade,

even if they could not compete in ship-building ; an example that now, when circumstances are reversed, we would
do well to imitate.   In wooden ship-building the proportion
of cost in material as compared with labor is far greater
than in iron ship-building.   The cost of plant is infinitely
less, and the cheapness of the wood compensates for the
difference of labor.   Finally, this part of the question may
be set at rest by considering the small demand there is now
for wooden ships for the great purposes of ocean commerce.

We cannot build iron and steel vessels as well as they are
built elsewhere, partly because competition is wanting.   We
need abundant foreign as well as the extremely limited home
competition that we have, in order to arouse the talent and
energy of our own ship-builders.

We cannot build ships as cheaply for reasons that the
ship-builders themselves assign.   Mr. Roach has repeatedly
stated that 90 per cent. of the cost of an iron steamship is
labor, and he has printed a table in one of his pamphlets
going to show that the cost of labor in this country is double
the cost of labor in Scotland.   The following schedule, intended as an argument for protection, from a recent number of *Our Continent*, purports to corroborate his statement
in the latter respect.   If both assumptions are strictly true,
your question is abundantly answered.

" COST OF SHIP-BUILDING IN ENGLAND AND AMERICA.

" In a ship-yard, to build an iron ship, thirty-six classes
of mechanics are employed, and these handle the raw material after it is made into shape.   Let them be divided, for
brevity's sake, into five departments, viz.: Ship-yard department, with fourteen different grades of employment ;
steam-engine department, numbering seven grades ; boiler
department, seven ;   iron and brass foundry department,
four grades each. - In the first department the highest wages
paid go to the shipsmith, and the lowest to the rivet boys.
In the United States the shipsmith receives, per week,

$15.95 ; in England $6.05 ; the rivet boy here gets $3.30, and abroad, $1.69. In the steam-engine department the draughtsman with us receives $19.80; in England he has $8.22. A helper in this department in this country gets $8.80; in England and in Scotland, $3.87. In the boiler department in the United States a flange-turner gets $16.50; the same man abroad gets $6.20. A loam moulder in the iron foundry here gets $16.50; in England, $6.50. Brass-moulders with us receive $14.30, and in England $6.15. The total week's wages of thirty-six men in England would be $192.60, while in the United States their wages would be $406.01. In a ship-yard, in good times, both here and in England, which might employ 2,000 men, they would receive in that case with us $22,540, and in England or on the Clyde only $10,700."

Of the cost of a $500,000 steamship, according to Mr. Roach's estimate, $450,000 would be for labor in England. The same labor here would cost $900,000 ! A manifest absurdity, and yet a logical deduction. Both statements are greatly exaggerated, while there is truth enough in them to meet your question. I once examined the books of Messrs. Denny and Co., the builders of the Parthia, Cunard's steamship of 3,000 tons, at Dumbarton, Scotland. Her cost was about £100,000 ($500,000).

There was 162,500 days' work done upon her, in which I do not include the manufacture of the iron from the pig, nor the making of the sailcloth, ropes, etc., but given the plates, angle iron, canvas, cordage, and all other materials as they come from the makers' hands ready to go into the composition of the ship.

At that time there was about a dollar in gold difference per day between the average Scotch and average American wages. Both have since increased, but the ratio of difference holds good. Of course, on account of our tariff, the iron as well as all other materials, excepting the wood used, cost considerably more here than in Scotland. But that is a matter of comparatively small account. There was only about 1,750 tons' weight of iron in that ship, and a few dollars' difference in its cost is a mere bagatelle when merged in $500,000.

Not considering it at all, then, the cost of such a ship if built here would be $162,500 more than if built in Scotland, besides which if the difference in cost of the iron *ab initio*, before it was wrought into plates, boiler iron, and angle iron, should be taken into account, it would amount to a great deal more. But putting the lowest estimate of difference, these figures show that it is more than 30 per cent. Yet in the face of his own superabundant calculations, and these more moderate ones, Mr. Roach has frequently stated that the difference in the whole cost of building a ship is only ten per cent. !

The only reply that has been made to this damaging summing up is that all the difference in the cost of ship-building, excepting about 10 per cent., is overcome by the superiority of American workmanship, the advantages of American iron, and improvements in American machinery. As to the first, it is well to bear in mind that it comes from a gentleman of Irish birth and raising, and that nearly all his employés are Irishmen or Scotchmen, many of them imported from the ship-yards of Great Britain. As for the superiority of American machinery, it is well to remember that in Great Britain there is neither a tariff on American iron nor on American ideas. If our iron would serve their purpose better than their own, the astute Scotsmen would surely import it, and where, in consequence of the competition among themselves, every labor-saving invention is eagerly adopted, we may be sure that no false national pride would prevent its introduction, even if it came from the Delaware.

One curious inconsistency is seen in the complaints of our ship-builders, who assert that there is only 10 per cent. against them, and at the same time deprecate the importation of free ships, the effect of which, as they say, very possibly with truth, would be to advance the price in Scotland 20 per cent. If they are correct in both premises, manifestly the American ship-builder would have an advantage over the Scotsman of 10 per cent., and again neither British law nor British pride would prevent Englishmen from supplying their necessities in the cheapest market, as they now do when they require wooden ships.

SECOND. *If we had such vessels without cost to us, could they be run by us in competition with those of other countries who build their own vessels and run them with their own officers and crews, without a modification or repeal of existing laws?*

ANSWER. I have to presume that this question is seriously put. When wooden sailing vessels were the carriers of the world, I have already shown that England so feared our competition that she repealed her restrictive navigation laws. We competed with her then in sailing ships under the same domestic disabilities that we now bear. I am not aware that our tonnage dues, which are the same as those levied on foreign vessels, were less then than now. We were obliged to pay duties on our stores and shipchandlery under various tariffs, all of them bad enough, though perhaps not quite so outrageous as the present imposition. We paid our captains and officers higher wages than other nations paid theirs, and we fed our ships' companies better. As to sailors, to the shame of a nation that engaged in a civil war for the freedom of Southern negroes, they are white slaves, everywhere bought of landlords in our seaports, who sell these chattels for the highest prices they can get to American and foreign vessels alike. So there is no difference there. As to taxation, in some States, notably New York and Massachusetts, we are better off now than we have ever been, for these States have passed laws exempting their shipping from taxation as personal property. In England it is not taxed as personal property, but its profits come under the income tax, which does not exist with us.

Our consular system is disgraceful. It always has been disgraceful, but it is no more so now than it ever was. It cannot be otherwise without an application of civil service reform, with continuance in office dependent on fitness and merit, and the payment of consular salaries out of the national treasury instead of out of the pockets of ship-owners. As to port dues and pilotage, embraced in the succeeding question, but forming also a part of the answer to this, they are no more than foreigners pay.

Lastly, in the days of wooden sailing ships, when we competed so advantageously with England, nobody proposed to *give* us ships. Like Englishmen, we were obliged to buy them. Therein is precisely the advantage that all foreigners have of us now. They can buy ships anywhere with their own money; we cannot. The ships would certainly be handsome presents if a generous government would give them to us. The interest, 6 per cent., and insurance, 7 per cent., on a steamship valued at $500,000 would amount to a saving of $65,000 annually, a sum large enough to pay all her port charges, pilotage, etc., at home, and leave a considerable residue for the benefit of our consuls abroad. But as this liberal offer is not likely to be made, we will be contented to pay our own bills.

Still, it would be desirable to have these petty charges modified. I have only intended to show that they are not the main impediments to our success.

I have demonstrated that we should be the gainers of $65,000 annually on every $500,000 ship which some fairy may be supposed to give us. Let us see how much we should save if we acquired the ship in England without supernatural aid.

Such a ship would cost here $650,000. The yearly interest and insurance on the excess of $150,000 is 13 per cent. The wear and tear and depreciation on an iron steamship is yearly at least 7 per cent. Therefore it would be 7 per cent. on this excess, making in all 20 per cent. on the $150,000, which would be $30,000.

Now, that amount, although less than half of the $65,000 we should gain in your supposed case, is still much more than enough in this real case to cover all the extra charges to which we are subjected, and of which so much complaint is made.

THIRD. *What modifications of existing laws or what new laws are required to remove discriminations against and burdens upon our shipping and ship-owning interests, such as customs dues, port dues, consular charges, pilotage, tonnage, and other dues, etc. ?*

ANSWER. I have already considered a part of this question. Please read sections 4131, 4132, 4133, 4134, 4135, 4142, 4143, 4163, 4165, 4172, of our navigation laws, and tell us if in the maritime code of any other nation anything can be found more barbarous and stultifying. What better can be done than to repeal them ?

FOURTH. *Compare the laws of other countries with our own with a view to their effect upon our and their shipping and ship-owning interests.*

ANSWER. To institute a minute comparison would be tedious and superfluous. In general, the laws of other countries give freedom to the carrying trade. Ours bind it in chains.

FIFTH. *Should our navigation laws be repealed or modified, and if modified, wherein and for what purpose ?*

ANSWER. Yes, for the good of the whole country they should be absolutely repealed ; but if ship-building for the coasting trade is still to be protected at the cost of the community, they should be merely so modified as to leave that virtually intact.

SIXTH. *What is the cost of the component materials of iron, steel, or wooden vessels in other countries and our own ?*

ANSWER. In general, the freight and duties added to their cost abroad will, with a small percentage of profit, indicate their price in this country.

SEVENTH. *What would be the effect of a rebate on any or all such materials ?*

ANSWER. It would, if ships were imported free, give the domestic ship-builder an opportunity to compete if he could ; but there is no more reason why there should be a rebate on parts of a ship than on a ship herself. Let both be made free.

EIGHTH. *Present any other statements connected with the cause of the decline of the American foreign carrying trade and what remedies can be applied by legislation.*

ANSWER. The sole reason for the decline of our carrying trade is the neglect of our Government to pursue the same liberal policy that other nations have adopted. No farmer can cultivate his ground as cheaply as his neighbor, unless he can have his implements of husbandry on as favorable terms. Let him make them if he can. If he cannot do so economically he must buy them, or his farm will not be a success.

Of all propositions for the restoration of our general carrying trade, the subsidy scheme would be the most ineffectual. It never has been adopted by any other nation for that purpose. It must be apparent to any unprejudiced mind that while subsidies may be needed for mail service, and for mail service only, the subsidized lines tend to prevent the business of private merchantmen by their ability to run them off. Subsidies are, therefore, for individual benefit, and necessarily opposed to the benefit of the public.

The means I would propose for the desired object are the same that I suggested to the Congressional Committee appointed in 1869, and have steadily adhered to from that time. They are as follows :

1st. The admission to American register of all vessels of over 3,000 tons.

2d. The admission of all materials to be used in the construction and repairs of vessels of over 3,000 tons, duty free.

3d. Exemption from taxation, local and national, on all vessels engaged in the foreign trade.

4th. Permission for all American vessels in the foreign trade to take their stores and shipchandlery out of bond duty free.

5th. A general revision of our laws relating to seamen, and also of those regulating consular service, so that the charges which now weigh in any degree on American shipping at home and in foreign ports may be diminished, and made to accord as far as possible with those imposed under the English system.

I have suggested a limited tonnage which will not materially interfere with the coasting trade, rather than the admission of ships to be used in the foreign trade exclusively.

The reason is that no Americans would wish to own ships whose voyages they could not control. · If they could not use them when they desired to do so in the coasting trade, they would prefer to own them as they own them now under the British flag, because it is more economical, and they are protected by a more efficient navy than ours.

In conclusion, I am sorry to express the opinion that, do what Congress will in the way of removing our burdens, even to the extent of granting absolute freedom and copying our navigation laws in all respects after those of England, measures that would have been eminently·successful in the outset, the restoration of our carrying trade will be a labor of years. We have lost our prestige and experience; we are no longer a maritime nation; our ship-owners have been wearied and disgusted; they have gone into other business, forced by their Government to abandon their old calling. And the way back under the most hopeful conditions must be uphill and slow. Our ship-masters, the pride of the ocean in the old packet days, are dead, and they have no successors. Congress, by its supine neglect, has all this for which to answer. While it has lent a listening ear to bounty and subsidy seekers intent only on personal gain, its committees have never been willing to report a free ship bill, nor has the Senate, or the House, allowed the subject to be otherwise than incidentally debated.

These, gentlemen, are sober truths, and I appeal to you now to rectify the errors of the past so far as it is in your power.

APPENDIX III.

In the Senate of the United States.—January 13, 1883. Read twice and referred to the Committee on Commerce February 23, 1883. Reported by Mr. Vest with amendments, viz. : Omit the parts struck through and insert the parts printed in *italics.*

An Act to remove certain burdens on the American merchant marine, to encourage the American foreign carrying trade, and to amend the laws relating to the shipment and discharge of seamen.

Be it enacted by the Senate and House of Representatives of the United States of America in Congress assembled, That section forty-one hundred and thirty-one of the Revised Statutes be amended so as to read as follows :

" Sec. 4131. Vessels registered pursuant to law, and no others, except such as shall be duly qualified according to law for carrying on the coast trade and fisheries, or one of them, shall be deemed vessels of the United States, and entitled to the benefits and privileges appertaining to such vessels ; but they shall not enjoy the same longer than they shall continue to be wholly owned by citizens and to be commanded by a citizen of the United States."

Sec. 2. That section forty-two hundred and nineteen of the Revised Statutes be amended by striking out the following words in the last clause : " And any vessel any officer of which shall not be a citizen of the United States shall pay a tax of fifty cents per ton."

Sec. 3. That section forty-five hundred and eighty of the Revised Statutes be amended so as to read as follows :

"Sec. 4580. Upon the application of any seaman to a consular officer for a discharge, if it appears to such officer that said seaman is entitled to his discharge under any act of Congress or according to the general principles or usages of maritime law as recognized in the United States, the officer shall discharge said seaman, and require from the master of said vessel, before such discharge shall be made, payment of the wages which may then be due said seaman. When a seaman is discharged by reason of inability to perform his duties, whether in consequence of illness or other causes, the master shall be required to pay him only the wages due at the time of discharge. But if any seaman is discharged in consequence of any hurt or injury received while in the service of the ship, or illness caused by a want of such food, water, accommodations, medicines, or anti-scorbutics as are required by law, the master shall be required to pay the expense of providing the necessary surgical and medical advice, with attendance and medicines, until said seaman is cured, or dies, or is brought back to some port in the United States."

Sec. 4. That section forty-five nundred and eighty-three of the Revised Statutes be amended so as to read as follows :

"Sec. 4583. No payment of extra wages shall be required, upon the discharge of any seaman in a foreign country upon the termination of his agreement, or by his own request, or in cases where vessels are wrecked or stranded, or condemned as unfit for service. If any consular officer, upon the complaint of any seaman that he has fulfilled his contract, or that the voyage is continued contrary to his agreement, is satisfied that the contract has expired, or that the voyage has not been continued by cir-

cumstances within the control of the master, he shall discharge the mariner; but in case the consular officer shall
be satisfied that the master has designedly continued the
voyage, he shall require from said master the payment of
one month's extra pay over and above the wages due at the
time of discharge; but in case the master of the vessel
shall provide said seaman with adequate employment on
board some other ship bound to the port at which he was
originally shipped, or to some other port, as may be agreed
upon by him, or furnish the means of sending him back to
such port, or provide him with a passage home, or deposit
with the consular officer such a sum of money as is by such
officer deemed sufficient to defray the expenses of his subsistence and passage home, then no payment of extra wages
shall be required."

SEC. 5. That section forty-five hundred and eighty-two
of the Revised Statutes be amended so as to read as
follows :

" Sec. 4582. Whenever a vessel belonging to a citizen of
the United States is sold in a foreign country, and her
company discharged, it shall be the duty of the master to
produce to the consul or officer the certified list of his
ship's company, and also the shipping articles, and to pay
to said consul or officer for every seaman so discharged one
month's pay over and above the wages which may then be
due to such seaman ; but in case the master of the vessel
so sold shall provide such seaman with adequate employment on board some other ship bound to the port at which
he was originally shipped, or to such other port as may be
agreed upon by him, or furnish the means of sending him
back to such port, or provide him with a passage home, or
deposit with the consular officer such a sum of money as is
by such officer deemed sufficient to defray the expenses of
his subsistence and passage home, then no payment of
extra wages shall be required."

SEC. 6. That section forty-six hundred of the Revised
Statutes be amended so as to read as follows :

"Sec. 4600. It shall be the duty of consular officers to reclaim deserters and discountenance insubordination by every means within their power, and where the local authorities can be usefully employed for that purpose, to lend their aid and use their exertions to that end in the most effectual manner. In all cases where deserters are apprehended consular officers shall inquire into the facts; and if he is satisfied that the desertion was caused by unusual or cruel treatment, the seaman shall be discharged, and receive in addition to his wages to the time of his discharge, one month's pay, or the master shall provide him with adequate employment on board some other ship bound to the port at which he was originally shipped, or to such other port as may be agreed upon by him, or furnish the means of sending him back to such port, or provide him with a passage. home, or deposit with the consular officer such a sum of money as is by such officer deemed sufficient to defray the expenses of his subsistence and passage home. And the officer discharging him shall enter upon the crew-list and shipping-articles the cause of discharge and the particulars in which the cruelty or unusual treatment consisted, and the facts as to his discharge, or re-engagement, as the case may be, and subscribe his name thereto officially."

SEC. 7. That section forty-five hundred and eighty-one of the Revised Statutes be amended so as to read as follows :

"Sec. 4581. That if any consular officer, when discharging any seaman, shall neglect to require the payment of and collect the extra wages and charges required to be paid in the case of the discharge of any seaman, he shall be accountable to such seaman to the full amount thereof; and if any seaman shall, after his discharge, have incurred any expense for board or other necessaries at the place of his discharge, before shipping again, such expense shall be paid out of the wages to which he shall be entitled, which shall be retained for that purpose, and the balance only paid over to him."

SEC. 8. That section forty-five hundred and eighty-four of the Revised Statutes be amended so as to read as follows:

" Sec. 4584. Whenever any consular officer, upon the discharge of any seaman, receives the wages due to said seaman, he shall at once pay the same to the said seaman, except as provided by section forty-five hundred and eighty-one of the Revised Statutes."

SEC. 9. That section forty-five hundred and seventy-eight of the Revised Statutes be amended so as to read as follows :

" Sec. 4578. All masters of vessels belonging to citizens of the United States and bound to some port of the same, are required to take such destitute seaman on board their vessels, at the request of the consuls, vice-consuls, commercial agents, or vice-commercial agents, respectively, and to transport them to the port in the United States to which such vessel may be bound, on such terms, not exceeding ten dollars for each person, as may be agreed between the master and the consul or officer. But for long voyages and peculiar disabled condition of such seamen, there shall be allowed to the master or owner of such vessel such reasonable compensation, not to exceed thirty cents per day, in addition to the allowances herein provided, as shall be deemed equitable by the collector of the port in the United States which the vessel may first reach, the same to be paid under such regulations as may be prescribed by the Secretary of the Treasury. Every such master who refuses the same, on the request or order of such consul or officer, shall be liable to the United States in a penalty of one hundred dollars for each seaman so refused. The certificate of any such consul or officer, given under his hand and official seal, shall be presumptive evidence of such refusal in any court of law having jurisdiction for the recovery of the penalty. No master of any vessel shall, however, be obliged to take a greater number than two men to every one hundred tons burden of the vessel on any one voyage."

SEC. 10. That no fees shall hereafter be charged by any consular officer for any certificate, manifest, or other official service to American vessels engaged in the foreign trade, or to the owners, officers, or seamen of such vessels. Consular officers who are now paid in whole or in part by fees shall make a detailed report to the Secretary of the Treasury of the services performed in accordance with this section, with the fees heretofore allowed in such cases, and shall be entitled to receive the amount thereof in the same manner as is provided by law in case of other compensation payable by the United States.

SEC. 11. That it shall be, and is hereby, made unlawful in any case to pay any seaman wages in advance of the time when he has actually earned the same, or to pay such advance wages to any other person, or to pay any person any remuneration for the shipment of seamen. Any person paying such advance wages or such remuneration shall be deemed guilty of a misdemeanor, and upon conviction shall be punished by a fine not less than four times the amount of the wages so advanced or remuneration so paid, and may be also imprisoned for a period not exceeding six months, at the discretion of the court. The payment of such advance wages or remuneration shall in no case absolve the steamer, ship, or vessel, or the master or owner thereof, from full payment of wages after the same shall have been actually earned, and shall be no defence to a libel, suit, or action for the recovery of such wages : *Provided*, That this section shall not apply to such fees as by any law of the United States may be collected by any shipping commissioner or other officer of the United States for the shipment of seamen : *And provided further*, That this section shall not apply to vessels engaged in the whaling business. This section shall apply as well to foreign vessels as to vessels of the United States ; and any foreign vessel the master, owner, consignee, or agent of which has violated this section, or induced or connived at its violation, shall be refused a clearance from any port of the United States. It shall be lawful, however, for any seaman to stipulate in his shipping agreement for the allotment of any portion of the wages which he may earn to his wife, father, mother, grandfather, grandmother, child, grandchild, brother, or sister, or to any savings bank for the benefit of such seaman, and to no other person or corporation.

SEC. 12. That every vessel mentioned in the preceding section shall also be provided with a slop-chest, which shall contain a complement of clothing for the intended voyage for each seaman employed, including boots or shoes, hats or caps, under clothing and outer clothing, oiled clothing, and everything necessary for the wear of a seaman; also a full supply of tobacco and blankets. Any of the contents of the slop-chest shall be sold, from time to time, to any or every seaman applying therefor, for his own use, at a profit not exceeding twenty-five per centum of the reasonable wholesale value of the same at the port at which the voyage commenced.

SEC. 13. That all masters and owners of vessels shall have the right to ship and pay off the men they employ, and that all laws or parts of laws requiring the payment of any remuneration to the shipping commission for the shipment of seamen, if shipped by said masters or owners, be, and the same are hereby repealed : Provided, That the duties performed by the shipping commissioner at home ports shall be performed by the collector of the several ports of the United States, and that no fee shall be charged for said services.

Sec. 14. That section twenty-five hundred and fourteen of the Revised Statutes be amended so as to read as follows :

" Sec. 2514. That all materials of foreign production to be manufactured in this country into articles needed for, and used in the construction, equipment, repairs, or supplies of American vessels employed, or to be employed, exclusively in the foreign trade, including the trade between the Atlantic ports and Pacific ports of the United States, may be withdrawn from bonded warehouse free of duty, under such regulations as the Secretary of the Treasury may prescribe; and if the duty shall have been already paid upon such material so used the same shall be refunded and repaid to the owner or owners of such vessels so using them or to their legal representatives."

SEC. 15. That in lieu of all duties on tonnage, including light money, now imposed by law, a duty of six cents per ton is hereby imposed at each entry on all vessels which shall be entered in the United States from the West India Islands, or from any port or place in the Republic of Mexico, or from any port or place south of Mexico, down to and including Aspinwall and Panama, or from any port or place in the Dominion of Canada ; and a duty of twelve cents per ton is hereby imposed at each entry on all vessels which shall be entered in the United States from any other foreign port : *Provided*, That nothing in this section shall be construed to repeal section twenty-seven hundred and ninety-three of the Revised Statutes : *And provided also*, That the aggregate duty imposed under this section in any one year upon any vessel engaged in no other foreign trade than the trade between the United States and the Dominion of Canada, or the Republic of Mexico, or any ports or places south of Mexico, down to and including Aspinwall and Panama, or any ports or places in the West India Islands, shall not exceed thirty cents per ton.

SEC. 16. That instead of the assessment of forty cents per month upon seamen engaged in the foreign carrying trade, authorized by sections forty-five hundred and eighty-five, and forty-five hundred and eighty-seven of the Revised Statutes of the United States, there shall hereafter be assessed and collected twenty cents.

SEC. 17. That the individual liability of a ship-owner shall be limited to the proportion of any or all debts and liabilities that his individual share of the vessel bears to the whole ; and the aggregate liabilities of all the owners of a vessel on account of the same shall not exceed the value of such vessels : *Provided,* That this provision shall not affect the liability of any owner incurred previous to the passage of this act, nor prevent any claimant from joining all the owners in one action ; nor shall the same apply to wages due to persons employed by said ship-owners.

SEC. 18. That when a steam or sailing vessel is built in the United States for foreign account, wholly or partly of foreign materials, on which import duties have been paid, there shall be allowed on such vessel, when exported, a drawback equal in amount to the duty paid on such materials, to be ascertained under such regulations as may be prescribed by the Secretary of the Treasury. Ten per centum of the amount of such drawback so allowed shall, however, be retained for the use of the United States by the collector paying the same.

SEC. 19. Whenever any fine, penalty, forfeiture, exaction, or charge arising under the laws relating to vessels or seamen has been paid under protest to any collector of customs or consular officer, and application has been made within one year from such payment of the refunding or remission of the same, the Secretary of the Treasury, if on investigation he finds that such fine, penalty, forfeiture, exaction, or charge was illegally, improperly, or excessively imposed, shall have the power, either before or after the same has been covered into the Treasury, to refund so much of such fine, penalty, forfeiture, exaction, or charge as he may think proper, from any moneys in the Treasury not otherwise appropriated.

SEC. 20. That Section twenty-nine hundred and sixty-six of the Revised Statutes be amended by striking out the words " propelled in whole or in part by steam ; " so that said section as amended shall read as follows :

" Sec. 2966. When merchandise shall be imported into any port of the United States from any foreign country in vessels, and it shall appear by the bills of lading that the merchandise so imported is to be delivered immediately after the entry of the vessel, the collector of such port may

15

take possession of such merchandise and deposit the same in bonded warehouse ; and when it does not appear by the bills of lading that the merchandise so imported is to be immediately delivered, the collector of the customs may take possession of the same and deposit it in bonded warehouse, at the request of the owner, master, or consignee of the vessel, on three days' notice to such collector after the entry of the vessel."

SEC. 21. That section twenty-eight hundred and seventy-two of the Revised Statutes be amended by adding thereto the following :

" When the license to unload between the setting and rising of the sun is granted to a sailing vessel under this section, a fixed, uniform, and reasonable compensation may be allowed to the inspector or inspectors for service between the setting and rising of the sun, under such regulations as the Secretary of the Treasury may prescribe, to be received by the collector from the master, owner, or consignee of the vessel, and to be paid by him to the inspector or inspectors."

Sec. 22. That section thirty-nine hundred and seventy-six of the Revised Statutes of the United States, and all other compulsory laws and parts of laws that oblige American vessels to carry the mails of the United States arbitrarily, or that prevent the clearance of vessels until they shall have taken mail matter on board, be, and the same are hereby, repealed ; and that section four thousand and nine of the Revised Statutes of the United States be, and is hereby, amended and re-enacted so as to read as follows, to wit :

" Sec. 4009. For transporting the mails of the United States between any port of the United States and any foreign port, or between ports of the Atlantic and ports in the Pacific, touching at any foreign port, a sum not exceeding one dollar per mile, on the trip each way, of actual nautical miles travelled between terminal points, for each trip actually made ; but such service shall be performed only under

contract entered into by the Postmaster-General, after legal advertisement, with the lowest responsible bidder, and the aggregate amount to be expended for such service shall not exceed one million five hundred thousand dollars per annum. The ships with which such contracts shall be made shall be ships of American registry only, and contracts shall be for a term of not less than four years ; and the general laws regulating the transportation of inland mails shall be applicable to such contracts, except as herein provided. And all vessels engaged in such contracts shall in time of war be subject to purchase or charter by the United States at reasonable rates ; and all foreign vessels or sailing vessels carrying the mails of the United States may be allowed a sum not exceeding the sea postage now allowed by law."

SEC. 23. That all acts and parts of acts in conflict with this act are hereby repealed.

Passed the House of Representatives January 12, 1883.

Attest : EWD. McPHERSON, *Clerk.*

APPENDIX IV.

NEW YORK, February 11, 1882.

LIEUT. CHARLES BELKNAP, U.S.N.,

   Secretary U. S. Naval Institute, Annapolis, Md, :

SIR—The undersigned having been requested to serve as Judges to determine to whom shall be awarded the gold medal and prize offered by the Naval Institute for the best essay on the subject " Our Merchant Marine : the Causes of its Decline, and the Means to be taken for its Revival," have examined eleven essays submitted in competition. Many of them have much merit ; but on a subject of the broad historical and practical nature of that submitted for competition, it will not be understood that in indicating any of them, the undersigned adopt as their own the entirety of the views therein presented, or the completeness of their conclusions either as to the causes of decline or the means for revival. They are prepared, however, to designate the essay under the motto *"Nil clarius aquis"* [1] as combining the most merit, and as worthy of the prize.

In accordance with the request that if there be another essay, or others, worthy of honorable mention, it be designated, or if more than one, they be mentioned in the order of merit, the undersigned designate the essay bearing the

---

[1] The essay designated by this motto forms that portion of the "Question of Ships " which treats of the restoration of the Merchant Marine, and was written by the Author.

motto " *Mais il faut cultiver notre jardin* " as second in the order of merit, and they further mention those bearing the respective mottoes " *Causa latet, vis est notissima* " and " *Spero meliora* " as worthy of honorable mention, without, however, being entirely agreed as to their comparative merits.

We are, sir, very respectfully yours,

HAMILTON FISH,
A. A. LOW,
J. D. JONES.

LIFE OF

Lord Lawrence

BY

R. BOSWORTH SMITH, M.A.,

LATE FELLOW OF TRINITY COLLEGE; ASSISTANT MASTER AT HARROW
SCHOOL.

With Maps and Portraits, 2 vols., 8vo, $5.00.

"As a biography, the work is an inthralling one, rich in anecdotes and incidents of Lord Lawrence's tempestuous nature and beneficent career that bring into bold relief his strongly-marked and almost colossal individuality, and rich also in instances of his courage, his fortitude, his perseverance, his self-control, his magnanimity, and in the details of the splendid results of his masterful and masterly policy. . . . We know of no work on India to which the reader can refer with so great certainty for full and dispassionate information relative to the government of the country, the characteristics of its people, and the fateful events of the forty eventful years of Lord Lawrence's Indian career."—*Harper's Magazine.*

"John Lawrence, the name by which the late Viceroy of India will always be best known, has been fortunate in his biographer, Mr. Bosworth Smith, who is an accomplished writer and a faithful, unflinching admirer of his hero. He has produced an entertaining as well as a valuable book; the general reader will certainly find it attractive; the student of recent history will discover in its pages matters of deep interest to him."—*London Daily Telegraph.*

** *For sale by all booksellers, or sent, post-paid, upon receipt of price, by*

CHARLES SCRIBNER'S SONS, PUBLISHERS,

743 AND 745 BROADWAY, NEW YORK.

MESSRS. CHARLES SCRIBNER'S SONS

publish, under the general title of

THE CAMPAIGNS OF THE CIVIL WAR,

A Series of volumes, contributed by a number of leading actors in and students of the great conflict of 1861-'65, with a view to bringing together, for the first time, a full and authoritative military history of the suppression of the Rebellion.

The final and exhaustive form of this great narrative, in which every doubt shall be settled and every detail covered, may be a possibility only of the future. But it is a matter for surprise that twenty years after the beginning of the Rebellion, and when a whole generation has grown up needing such knowledge, there is no authority which is at the same time of the highest rank, intelligible and trustworthy, and to which a reader can turn for any general view of the field.

The many reports, regimental histories, memoirs, and other materials of value for special passages, require, for their intelligent reading, an ability to combine and proportion them which the ordinary reader does not possess. There have been no attempts at general histories which have supplied this satisfactorily to any large part of the public. Undoubtedly there has been no such narrative as would be especially welcome to men of the new generation, and would be valued by a very great class of readers ;—and there has seemed to be great danger that the time would be allowed to pass when it would be possible to give to such a work the vividness and accuracy that come from personal recollection. These facts led to the conception of the present work.

From every department of the Government, from the officers of the army, and from a great number of custodians of records and special information everywhere, both authors and publishers have received every aid that could be asked in this undertaking; and in announcing the issue of the work the publishers take this occasion to convey the thanks which the authors have had individual opportunities to express elsewhere.

The volumes are duodecimos of about 250 pages each, illustrated by maps and plans prepared under the direction of the authors.

The price of each volume is $1.00.

The following volumes are now ready:

I.—*The Outbreak of Rebellion.* By JOHN G. NICOLAY, Esq., Private Secretary to President Lincoln ; late Consul-General to France, etc.

A preliminary volume, describing the opening of the war, and covering the period from the election of Lincoln to the end of the first battle of Bull Run.

VIII.—*The Mississippi.* By Francis Vinton Greene, Lieut. of Engineers, U. S. Army; late Military Attaché to the U. S. Legation in St. Petersburg; Author of "The Russian Army and its Campaigns in Turkey in 1877–78," and of "Army Life in Russia."

An account of the operations—especially at Vicksburg and Port Hudson—by which the Mississippi River and its shores were restored to the control of the Union.

IX.—*Atlanta.* By the Hon. Jacob D. Cox, Ex-Governor of Ohio; late Secretary of the Interior of the United States; Major General U. S. V., commanding Twenty-third Corps during the campaigns of Atlanta and the Carolinas, etc., etc.

From Sherman's first advance into Georgia in May, 1864, to the beginning of the March to the Sea.

X.—*The March to the Sea—Franklin and Nashville.* By the Hon. Jacob D. Cox.

From the beginning of the March to the Sea to the surrender of Johnston—including also the operations of Thomas in Tennessee.

XI.—*The Shenandoah Valley in 1864. The Campaign of Sheridan.* By George E. Pond, Esq., Associate Editor of the *Army and Navy Journal.*

XII.—*The Virginia Campaign of '64 and '65. The Army of the Potomac and the Army of the James.* By Andrew A. Humphreys, Brigadier General and Bvt. Major General, U. S. A.; late Chief of Engineers; Chief of Staff, Army of the Potomac, 1863–64; commanding Second Corps, 1864–'65, etc., etc.

Statistical Record of the Armies of the United States. By Frederick Phisterer, late Captain U. S. A.

This Record includes the figures of the quotas and men actually furnished by all States; a list of all organizations mustered into the U. S. service; the strength of the army at various periods; its organization in armies, corps, etc.; the divisions of the country into departments, etc.; chronological list of all engagements, with the losses in each; tabulated statements of all losses in the war, with the causes of death, etc.; full lists of all general officers, and an immense amount of other valuable statistical matter relating to the War.

The complete Set, thirteen volumes, in a box. Price, $12.50
Single volumes, ... 1.00

*** *The above books for sale by all booksellers, or will be sent, post-paid, upon receipt of price, by*

CHARLES SCRIBNER'S SONS, Publishers,

743 and 745 Broadway, New York.

THE
CAMPAIGNS OF THE CIVIL WAR.

OPINIONS OF THE PRESS ON THE SERIES.

From the CINCINNATI COMMERCIAL.

" Scribner's Campaigns of the Civil War are probably the ablest and most striking account of the late war that has yet been written. Choosing the flower of military authors, the publishers have assigned to each the task of writing the history of the events he knew most about. Thus, both accuracy and a life-like freshness have been secured."

From the HARTFORD POST.

" No series of books has awakened so much discussion in years as the campaign volumes which the New York publishers are now providing for the public. To the veterans who served in the war the works are of the deepest concern and have been read with profound interest."

From the BOSTON ADVERTISER.

" We can only call attention here once more to the excellent plan of this new history of the war, and the fidelity and care with which the several writers have performed their tasks. * * * That which has been now done by the authors of ' The Campaigns ' will never need to be done again."

From the UTICA (N. Y.) HERALD.

"As this series approaches its close the reader is compelled to testify that it has already become the standard history of the war of the rebellion as a whole, and it will be long, if ever, before any rival can supplant it."

From the N. Y. CHRISTIAN ADVOCATE.

" The altogether admirable series on the ' Campaigns of the Civil War ' draws near completion. We doubt if a better and more evenly sustained series can be found on any subject. More than any other work, this will be the trusted history of our civil war,"

From the New York TRIBUNE.

"A high degree of editorial tact and intelligence characterizes the execution of Messrs. Scribner's excellent undertaking. The division of the work is judicious ; the allotment of topics to the various writers is happy, and cordial co-operation has been secured from recognized authorities, from the Government, from distinguished military officers, and from the custodians of public and private records. To all this we may add that the volumes are convenient in size, beautifully printed, and furnished with many clear and simple maps."

CHARLES SCRIBNER'S SONS, PUBLISHERS,
743 AND 745 BROADWAY, NEW YORK.

www.ingramcontent.com/pod-product-compliance
Lightning Source LLC
Chambersburg PA
CBHW030812020726
47499CB00006B/1876